The Butcher

Fifth Republic Series
Book 1

Penelope Sky

Hartwick Publishing

Hartwick Publishing

The Butcher

Copyright © 2025 by Penelope Sky

All rights reserved.

Contents

1. Fleur   1
2. Fleur   37
3. Bastien   47
4. Fleur   81
5. Bastien   93
6. Fleur   107
7. Bastien   111
8. Fleur   113
9. Fleur   123
10. Bastien   140
11. Fleur   164
12. Bastien   195
13. Fleur   216
14. Bastien   252
15. Fleur   273

Chapter 1

Fleur

I entered the building, walked up the five flights of stairs because the elevator had been busted since I moved in, and then got my key in the lock. The door opened, and I entered my small apartment, the one-bedroom flat with a kitchen that also served as a laundry room. I flicked on the light switch and then gave a small jump at the sight of the man sitting in the armchair like a goddamn gargoyle. "Jesus..." I gave my keys a squeeze before I tossed them on the table and set my purse down. "I told you to stop doing that."

He continued to sit there with his elbows on his knees, his shoulders broad in his jacket, his eyes down on his fingers as he gripped his phone. It took him a moment to lift his chin and look at me, his hazelnut eyes full of self-loathing. "If you don't want me here, then pick up your fucking phone."

1

"I don't have to do anything, Adrien." It was nearly two in the morning, but the City of Lights still had people on every corner, riding their bikes to the opposite side of town or smoking in the cafés downstairs. *Au Pied de Cochon* was right near my apartment, one of the few restaurants in Paris that basically never locked their doors or turned off their lights because it was open almost twenty-four hours. I'd eaten there a couple times after my shift, but mostly just to wind down with a cigarette.

He rose to his feet, in dark jeans and a leather jacket, raindrops visible on the material like it had sprinkled on him during his walk from the car. He left the green armchair and came close to where I stood by the round dining table, which held a vase full of flowers that I'd grabbed from the market yesterday. "I found a marriage counselor—"

"I don't want to go to counseling," I snapped. "I want a divorce." I'd asked for a divorce the moment I'd discovered his infidelity, a treason he didn't even have the balls to tell me himself. But he'd made that request impossible to grant. Made me jump through endless hoops, just to get rejected by the court—because he'd paid everyone off.

"We're Catholic. We don't believe in divorce—"

"So you fucked around under the assumption I would never leave?"

"That's not what I mean."

"I don't want to make this marriage work. I'm a fine piece of ass who doesn't need this shit. I want a man who keeps his word and is so brutally honest that it's almost cruel. You are not that man, Adrien."

The anger flickered across his face, but he tightened the reins on his rage. "I made a mistake. I told you it wasn't an affair. She meant nothing to me."

"But she was worth your marriage?"

His nostrils flared, but he still didn't yell like he normally would. "There was a lot of shit going on at work and I had too much wine to drink, and she came on to me. I had a moment of weakness. I'm fucking human."

I rolled my eyes. "More like a Neanderthal."

His desperate eyes were locked on mine. "I said I was sorry about a million times."

"I don't want an apology. I want a divorce. I want you to stop popping up in my apartment like you still own me."

"You're still my wife—"

"Fuck you."

He drew in a slow breath and closed his eyes briefly. "You wouldn't be this angry if you didn't still love me."

"I'm just an angry person, Adrien."

"You're a passionate person, Fleur. There's a difference," he said. "It happened once, and it won't happen again. I will do anything you want to make this work because, despite what you think, I love you with everything I have."

I stepped away because I didn't want to look at him anymore. Rain started to pelt the windows and the skylight above the kitchen. The curtains were open, and the light from the lampposts illuminated the city and the wet pavement in the rain.

"Fleur."

I kept my back to him.

"I'll never give you a divorce. Every time you submit your paperwork, the judge will deny it. You will never remarry because your marriage to me will remain intact. The only way I'll lift those restrictions is if you try to make this work."

I continued to look out the window.

"If you work on this marriage with me."

I crossed my arms over my chest, and I felt the cold from the windowpane. I could see my reflection as a faint outline. The city below was so beautiful, but it was hard to appreciate it when I felt so low. I never shed a tear in

4

front of him. I turned to the feeling that was the easiest to feel—which was anger. "Were there others?"

"No." His answer was quick, almost too quick.

I turned around and faced him, studying his hard eyes. His hair was dark like espresso, and his eyes were warm like hazelnut. His Italian ancestry was visible on his skin, and he spoke both French and Italian, one of the things that had attracted me to him. Marriage was such a profound experience that changed everything, and my marriage had left all kinds of scars. Even when we were so far apart, I still felt attached to him. But I didn't want to be attached to him. "Were there others?"

His eyes flinched slightly when I asked the question again, a subtle hesitation. "No."

I studied his face, searching for a hint of a lie and unsure how to decipher what I saw. But I knew that I shouldn't even have to ask the question, that I shouldn't have to wonder if it was a lie or the truth. "I need to think."

"There was no one else—"

"I need space, Adrien. Stop blowing up my phone and lurking in my apartment like a goddamn stalker so I can have two seconds to think." I turned back to the window and watched a water drop streak to the bottom and disappear.

He lingered for a moment, his eyes hot on my spine, but then his feet eventually shifted and he left the apartment, taking as long as possible, as if I might ask him to come back.

I was a bartender at Silencio, a bar that was a thirty-minute walk from my apartment. I never took a taxi, even when I got off work at almost three in the morning, because it was just too expensive. And there was nothing more peaceful than walking Paris at night—especially in the rain.

It was a busy night at the bar, lots of people in the main room and dispersed throughout the other lounges. Waitresses would wait on those people and bring them drinks and small bites. I stayed at the bar and helped the people waiting for a table. At the beginning of the night, it was usually young people who'd just gotten off work and needed a drink after a stressful day. As the night passed, it turned into romantic dates. And then around midnight, different characters came in, rich men who wanted a place to drink in peace.

I'd adopted a habit of constantly scanning down the bar to see if anyone else needed a drink, and while my gaze wandered, I spotted him come through the door.

I gripped a bottle by the neck and halted where I stood. *Holy fuck.*

The second he entered the room, he disturbed the air around him. I wasn't sure what I noticed first, the fact that he was tall as fuck or hot as fuck. He had to be at least six foot three, but that might have been a conservative guess. He wore only a black t-shirt even though it was a rainy night, and he filled it out better than any mannequin at the mall. Thick shoulders and muscular arms, the kind that had veins so strained they looked like they were about to pop. He carried himself like he was important but also with an I-don't-give-a-fuck attitude. He had black ink everywhere, visible on both of his arms and on his hands, and even up his neck to his jawline. I'd never felt any particular way about tattoos, but I'd also never seen a man wear them so well.

He seemed to be alone because he moved to the only vacant chair before he took a seat, and the light from the bar behind me illuminated his beautiful and rugged face. I'd only been working at Silencio for a couple weeks, so perhaps he was a regular I'd never encountered before.

I continued to stand there with my fingers on the neck of the bottle, the rest of the patrons at the bar absorbed in conversation, my attention on the man who made my hair stand on end just because he'd stepped into my space.

The only pretty feature about him was his eyes. Crystal blue, like the waters along the white shores of a tropical paradise, more brilliant than the sky on a clear day. But the rest of his face was harsh, with sharp cheekbones, a jawline that could cut glass, and a mouth that looked like it could do more damage than a bullet from a gun.

His elbow rested on the counter as his fingers gently grazed his jawline, veins popping. He glanced at the menu that sat there but didn't seem to read it, like he already knew what he wanted. Then his eyes shifted to me, the confidence so striking it was like staring straight into the sun.

Oh my lord.

I was still holding the neck of a wine bottle, and I finally returned it to its holder behind the bar and walked over, my heart like a frog in my throat, so intimidated by his appearance that I wasn't sure if I could wait on him. "What can I get you?" It took all my strength not to stumble over my words, not to make a complete idiot out of myself and just act natural.

He stared at me for a solid three seconds, his blue eyes not needing to blink, having way more confidence than I did. "Scotch, on the rocks. Make it a double."

"You got it." I pulled out the bottle and made the drink.

He didn't watch my hands as I prepared the drink. Stared straight at my face. Still didn't blink.

I presented the drink to him. "Lemme know when you need another. I'll be around." I turned so I wouldn't see his reaction, knowing I needed to put as much distance between us as possible. He was so distracting that I wouldn't be able to finish up my shift if I continued to look at him. The fantasies were already passing through my mind, and I told myself it was only because it'd been a while since I had any dick.

But I had a feeling I'd never had any dick like that.

———

The bar started to grow quiet as people left for the night. He ordered another scotch and drank it alone at the bar, the chairs empty on either side of him. He didn't distract himself looking at his phone, just stared at his reflection in the mirror against the wall or stared off into the distance. He seemed perfectly fine drinking alone, not having anyone to talk to or anywhere to go. It didn't seem like he was there to pick up a woman for the night because he never looked at anyone in the room.

I wanted him to leave so I could finally release the breath I held, but I also dreaded the moment he walked out of that bar and I never saw him again. I stood at the counter and wiped off the bottles, doing my cleanup during the downtime so I could get out of there quicker after we closed.

"Bastien."

My eyes flicked to him, my heart in my throat again.

He took a drink then licked his lips. "This is where you tell me your name."

He was just as arrogant as I pegged him to be—but still hot as fuck. "Fleur."

He extended his empty glass, silently asking for another.

If he were someone else, I would have cut him off, but despite all the scotch he drank, he didn't seem even remotely incapacitated. He was either a functional drunk or his tolerance was sky-high. I poured another drink and placed it in front of him.

He raised his glass in a gesture of gratitude before he took a sip. His striking eyes were glued to mine, having the confidence to hold an intimate level of eye contact like we were lovers when we were strangers. He cocked his head slightly, as if he saw something in my stare. "There's a story behind those eyes."

"Is there a story behind yours?"

A subtle smile moved over his lips, and that little shift changed his entire face. The arrogance dulled in his eyes, and it was replaced by a hint of playfulness. He shook the ice in his glass before he took a drink. "Definitely." He returned it to the counter and stared at it for a second before he looked at me again. "You first."

Normally, when men made a pass at me, I flirted back in a restrained way, wanting them to have a good time and for me to get a good tip. But I was never honest about who I was or what I felt. But when I looked into those blue eyes, the truth was pulled out of me. "I'm in the middle of a divorce—sorta."

"Sorta?"

"I've tried filing the paperwork multiple times, but it's always rejected."

A sharpness entered his gaze, and his fingers moved over the top of his glass.

"He's well-connected to powerful people." I answered the question he never asked. "And he'll put me through hell to get away from him."

"Power and wealth go hand in hand," he said. "So why are you working here?"

"Because I don't want his money. I was poor before him, and I can be poor after him." It had been a harsh change, not having a driver to take me where I needed to go, getting my own groceries and carrying them up the stairs, having to do my own laundry and make sure I didn't turn the heater too high. Otherwise, I wouldn't be able to afford the bill. But it was still better than a life of luxury with a liar.

He continued to stare at me, his eyes narrowing in interest. "I could ask what prompted you to run, but I think I already know the answer." He shook the glass and took another drink. "Men say women are complicated, but they aren't. Just text back, and don't stick your dick in other people. Pretty straightforward."

I abandoned my cleanup at the bar because I'd become engrossed in this deep conversation with a stranger, feeling a connection to someone I didn't know. "Are you in a relationship?"

"No." He looked at me head on, having so much confidence it was nearly toxic. "I don't text back, and I like to stick my dick in a lot of places." He drank from his glass without breaking the connection with our eyes.

I felt no disappointment because that was exactly what I'd expected from him. If he was trying to pick me up, he wasn't doing it in a sleazy way. He was brutally honest, that if we left the bar together, I wouldn't hear from him again. He would probably be gone before I woke up in the morning. But honesty was a trait that I valued the instant I realized my marriage lacked it. "He wasn't the one to tell me. I had to hear it from her."

He didn't cast judgment or voice an opinion. Just stared at me and listened.

"He's been trying to get me back. Tightens his grip when he feels me slip further away."

"How long have you been married?"

"A couple years."

He gave a slight nod. "That's not a good sign. Who was the woman?"

"Someone he works with. Said it didn't mean anything."

Both of his elbows went to the bar as he leaned forward, cupping his knuckles in the other hand, the muscles and cords visible up and down his arms.

"I asked if there were others... He said no."

"You believe him?"

"I—I don't know." Every time I thought about what he'd done, I felt so shitty that I wanted to curl into a ball in the corner. It disgusted me, thinking about where his dick had been before it pounded inside me like there had never been any treason.

He continued to watch me, rubbing his knuckles like they were sore from a recent brawl.

"Have any advice?"

He lowered his hands to the counter, taller than me even when he sat down because he had a foot and a half of height on me. "I don't give advice—just opinion."

"Okay, then. What's your opinion?"

A subtle smile moved on to his lips as his eyes flicked away for the first time. "You don't want my opinion, sweetheart."

I hated it when men called me that, when they tried to get my attention from across the bar with the endearment, but Bastien pulled it off like it was my actual name. "I want honesty, and that's something I haven't gotten in a while."

His eyes came back to me and stayed there for a long time, studying my face like he could see words in bold ink across my skin. He tilted his head slightly before he released a sigh. "Trust is like glass. It takes time to heat and temper, to make it transparent for both parties to see through. But once it's shattered, there are so many broken pieces on the floor that it's impossible to put back together. A year may pass, and you'll step into the kitchen barefoot for a glass of water and get a shard in your heel. And you'll remember how it got there."

A pain settled on my heart, an anchor lowered from a ship, a disappointment so heavy it dropped to the bottom of the ocean.

"Power and wealth can be taken away—and all that's left is your word. If you don't have that, then you don't have anything. He betrayed his word when he betrayed you, so he betrayed himself. There was a chance of redemption by being honest with you, but he chose cowardice instead."

I hadn't expected this beautiful man at the bar to have so much depth, to be more than a pretty face with a stiff drink in his hand.

"He tells you there was no one else, but because his word is invalid, you don't know if you can believe him. A man should treat a woman with the same respect he treats his boys. If anything, she should be his number one guy."

"You make it sound like you've been in a relationship before."

"No." His hand rested on the top of his glass. "And that's why I haven't been in one. I know what it takes—and I haven't found a woman worth the effort. Probably never will. Not that I'm looking anyway." He stared at me as he took a drink from his glass. "So what are you going to do?"

"I'm not sure if I have much of a choice." Adrien would never stop, constantly blocking any motion to legally separate, showing up at my work and my apartment, as if I would find his persistence charming when fidelity was far more romantic.

"You always have a choice."

"You don't know my husband."

"But I know men." He gave me a hard stare. "And I know how to get rid of yours."

"How?"

He shifted his position on the stool, his shirt gripping his muscles with the movement, cords visible up his neck despite the ink that covered his skin. He had a skull right at the center of his throat, a dagger up the right side of his neck, the edge of the blade right at his jawline. "Fuck someone."

Heat from a roaring fire burst inside me, picturing him as the one doing all the fucking. Buck naked and deep inside me, his fat dick making me come with minimal effort. I knew he had a big dick because of the big dick energy he'd brought into the bar when he'd first walked in.

"No man can see past his ego, and he seems no different to me."

"What about you? Do you have a big ego?"

He smirked. "I wouldn't be a man if I didn't." He took another drink, making the glass empty with the exception of the ice cubes that hadn't melted yet. "I'll take the tab, sweetheart."

It was the time for him to make his move, but I suspected the offer would never come. He was the magnet that drew everyone in. He didn't need to chase anyone. Just sit there and wait for all the pretty girls to come to him.

I moved down the bar to the computer and generated his tab, putting in all the drinks that would have put a normal man flat on the floor. But before I could print the tab, I glanced to the other side of the room and instinctively knew something wasn't right.

Three men entered the bar, moving far too fast if all they wanted was a drink. And they had handkerchiefs tied over the bottom half of their faces to hide their identities from the cameras in all the corners.

Frozen to the spot, all I could do was stand there and watch one of them come at me—with a fucking machete.

He held up the machete at eye level. "Cash in the bag." He tossed a burlap sack on the counter. The other two men also had their machetes out, watching everyone else in the bar to make sure no one came to my rescue.

I stilled on the spot, struggling to breathe through the sheer panic.

"Bitch, fill the bag."

I didn't gasp or scream, but I was frozen to the spot in sheer terror.

"You picked the wrong bar, man."

My eyes glanced at Bastien, who remained on the stool. Everyone else at the bar had scurried to the wall. The other people in the seating area had tried to crawl under their tables or put their shaking arms in the air. Bastien was the only one who regarded the situation with an insane level of calm.

The man turned his attention to Bastien, taking the heat and the knife off me. "What'd you say, asshole?"

"I'm not the one threatening a girl with a knife, *asshole*." He left the stool and stood upright, and he seemed to grow several inches taller from when he had walked inside. He brandished no weapon other than his words, but he was still armed to the teeth with invisible power. "*Homines ex codice.*"

My eyes flicked back and forth between them, having no idea what was transpiring.

The words were in Latin, but the meaning was unclear. I couldn't tell if my assailant understood what that meant or if he was just as bewildered as I was.

There was a silent standoff between them, a tension that rose like flames from a newly lit bonfire. The bar was normally loud and boisterous with chatter and laughter, but now it'd gone deadly quiet—like a graveyard.

The asshole with the machete moved, slashing his weapon down like he would hack Bastien to pieces.

I screamed in terror and moved for one of the empty bottles behind the counter.

It happened so fast that I wasn't sure exactly what transpired, but Bastien made the other man's face bloody and wrested the machete free. He slammed the guy's face down on the counter, not once but twice—and broke his nose. He pinned his head to the top of the counter and looked at me. "Your turn, sweetheart."

I slammed the bottle down on his head, and it shattered into pieces.

"Nice swing." Bastien let go, and the man dropped to the floor in a pile of broken glass and blood.

The other two rushed to the door to split when shit got real, but Bastien got there first and punched one so hard in the face he slammed into the wall and collapsed on the floor. He made a series of moves on the other guy, blocking the arm holding the machete before slamming his elbow straight into his head and knocking him out cold.

When he was done, a strained silence enveloped the bar, everyone still too afraid to move or speak.

Bastien walked across the hardwood floor and the broken glass, back to the counter where I stood. He pulled out his wallet and rifled through the euros that were stuffed into it, and as if nothing serious had just happened, he asked, "What do I owe you?"

The bar closed and the police came. They asked Bastien a couple of questions, but it seemed like they already knew him because they didn't ask who he was. In fact, they treated him like a superior.

I stepped outside into the cold, the air wet from a drizzle that had just passed through. The pavement was wet from the recent rainfall, and a few people were on the street because no one ever slept in this city.

Bastien came outside a moment later and looked me over. "You alright?"

"A little frazzled, but I'm fine."

He continued to stare me down with those piercing blue eyes. "It's okay not to be fine."

My eyes flicked away, touched by the softness he was showing when he had been so ruthless a moment ago. "I know it is."

"Where's your apartment?"

I normally wouldn't give out my address to a stranger, but he somehow felt like anything but a stranger even though I only knew his first name. "Rue Coquilliere. By the Louvre."

"I'll walk you."

"I'm okay—"

"Come on." He took the lead, stepping into the empty street under the bright lampposts, moving past a building that had stood the test of time and survived the Second World War. "We have a conversation to finish."

We walked down the wet pavement together, side by side, but nothing was really said. He seemed to be a long-term resident of the city because he knew exactly where he was going, knew exactly what street to take without looking at his phone for guidance.

"How long have you lived in Paris?"

"All my life. You?"

"Same."

That was the extent of our conversation. We passed *Loup* on the corner and walked down the path where the restaurants were located beneath my apartment. There was a small road for cars, but only taxis pulled up to the area. Right now, it was deserted, all the restaurants closed except for *Au Pied de Cochon*.

He seemed to know it was one of the few restaurants open all hours of the day because he checked in with the host and asked for a table outside. The second we sat down, he lit up a cigar and blew the smoke into the air. We were the only ones outside because it was either too cold or too late.

He offered me a cigar.

"No thanks." I reached into my purse and pulled out a

pack of cigarettes. I lit up and felt the hit of nicotine the second the smoke hit my lungs.

He gave a subtle smile before he held his cigar between his fingertips. "You don't strike me as a smoker."

"I quit a couple years ago."

"But carry a pack wherever you go." He returned the cigar to his mouth and pulled in a puff before he let it out from his nostrils.

My eyes narrowed but in a playful way. "You are an asshole."

His smirk widened.

"I started up again once I moved out."

The playfulness evaporated, and he gave a slight nod in understanding.

"It's always been my vice."

"Everyone has their poison. No shame in that."

"Yes, but I want to live to see middle age at least."

He looked at the street as people passed, only a person every now and then, coming from the mall far down the way.

"You don't worry about that?"

He let the smoke leave his mouth before he answered. "No."

"Why?"

"I don't expect to live long—nor do I desire it." When he spotted the waitress in the window, he waved her over. "I'll take a scotch on the rocks. And whatever she's having."

I ordered my drink, and she left.

The last thing he said hadn't left my mind. "Why do you feel that way?"

He looked as he let the cigar rest between his fingertips, and the strength of his stare seemed to be his answer—or lack thereof.

I didn't press the question again, remembering we'd met just a few hours ago and I wasn't entitled to such personal information. "Are you a cop?"

A smile that lit up all his features hit his face, and when he chuckled, it came from deep in his chest. "No."

"It seemed like they knew you."

"Oh, they know me."

"But you aren't a cop."

He gave a slight shake of his head. "There are more than

cops and bandits. The food web is a lot bigger than most people realize."

"And where do you fit in this food web?"

He took another puff of his cigar. The waitress came out and brought our drinks before she returned to the warmth inside the restaurant. He glanced out at the darkness and the sycamore trees that lined the sidewalk before he looked at me again. "At the top."

I didn't consider my husband to be a criminal because he didn't kill people, but he made his money in less than notable ways. He and his guys stole famous pieces of art and replaced them with fakes because they sold the originals on the black market for a pretty penny. There were men out there with real van Goghs, da Vincis, and Michelangelos in their bathrooms—while the museums had counterfeits. Now I suspected Bastien was on a whole different—and dangerous—level. "The less I know, the better."

"Smart girl." He released the smoke from his mouth and let it float on the cool air. "And you've got a steely spine too. I like that."

"How so?"

"Most women would just put up with a man's infidelity so they could live in a big house and drive a nice car. But not you. You're an idealist, a woman of great moral character, who knows she's worth more than a man's bullshit. That's hot."

I held his stare but felt the warmth in my cheeks. Everyone I knew had told me to take Adrien back, that it was a one-time mistake and I should fight for the marriage. While there were times I considered it, letting it go didn't sit right with me.

"And you held your ground with that asshole. Didn't scream or cry."

"Make no mistake, I was fucking scared."

"But you didn't show it." He lowered the cigar and gave me a harder stare than he had before, full of authority and command. "And that's what matters. You reached for that wine bottle with every intention to kill—and you swung." He took a drink, wiped a drop from the corner of his mouth with his thumb, and then smiled. "And that's fucking hot."

My apartment was right next to Poppy Café, so literally just a few feet away from the restaurant. He walked me to the front door, painted green with two trees in planters on either side. It required a code to come and go, and the door weighed at least one hundred pounds and required two hands every time I had to open or close it.

He stopped several feet away from the door like he had no intention of coming inside. "Are you going to keep working at Silencio?"

I needed the job to keep the apartment, so I couldn't just quit the second things got rough. Another aspect of poverty that I didn't enjoy. "It can't get robbed a second time, right?"

"Then I'll see you next time, Fleur." He turned away, the pathway lined with tall bushes in planters.

"Bastien."

He turned back around, his blue eyes bright even from a distance in the dark, the sexiest man ever to have set foot on this road. One look at him showed he was dangerous, but that only made it harder to look away.

"You said there was a story behind my eyes. What's the story behind yours?" Maybe it was just lust that bound me to him, but I didn't want to let him go. Didn't want him to slip away in the night and disappear like a phantom that was never real in the first place. He was a man so hard but with such contradictory beauty, one who could speak the truth with a cruelty that hurt in a way that felt good.

His hands slid into his pockets as he looked at me, his shoulders shifting with the movement and showing a hint of the cut muscles underneath. "Are you inviting me inside, sweetheart?"

My entire body came alive at the prospect, the first rush of excitement I'd felt in months. Once I'd found out about Adrien's infidelity, I'd fallen into a depression so deep, it didn't have a bottom. But I stopped my fall and gripped the ledge, prepared to begin the climb back up. "Yes."

A smile didn't move across his face as I expected. It was the first time he looked at me like an opponent rather than an equal, with an unequivocal expression of warning in his steel-like gaze. "If you let me into your apartment, I'll throw your ass on the bed. I'll choke you. I'll spank you so hard my handprint will still be on your ass in the morning. You've been warned." He continued his stare, pulling off that statement in a way no other man ever could, and it had the intended effect because I was both scared—and fucking turned on.

So turned on, I had bumps on my arms, felt my mouth go dry, and sensed a throb down below. I held up my phone to the screen to scan the code so the door would unlock. I opened it, the hinges screaming from the weight, and then I looked at him. "Let's see if you're a man of your word."

The second the apartment door was shut behind us, he was on me, pinning me against the wall in the hallway, pushing up my top and bra so my tits would come out.

He gripped my ass with his big hands and lifted me, my back to the wall, and he sealed his mouth over mine for a kiss that nearly ripped my soul from my body.

He could hold me with a single arm because he seemed like he must lift tractors in the gym. He didn't slide his free hand into my hair but gripped one of my tits, squeezed it hard, and he flicked his thumb over my nipple, kissing me at the same time, a kiss that took the lead as I followed.

I grabbed his shirt and started to pull it over his head, having a hard time getting it off because he was all over me, kissing me so deeply I lost my train of thought, his hand squeezing my tit so hard I almost released a yelp. He was too into me to care about his clothing, so it took another tug to get it over his head and reveal what was underneath.

"Jesus Christ..." He was built. He was ripped. He had the single sexiest physique I'd ever seen—and I'd slept with some hot guys. He was so tight that cords on his body popped everywhere. I could see the definition of every muscle, the details of his body underneath the skin, the muscles hard enough to be armor. He had ink over his skin, black ink that showed death and misery and darkness, but it only enhanced just how hot he was. "You're so fucking hot—"

His mouth silenced my words with another kiss as he pinned me against the wall, his hand squeezing my ass through my jeans. He carried me down the hallway into the bedroom, the foot of the bed visible from the doorway. Just as he promised, he fucking threw me on the mattress.

I landed and rolled onto my stomach, my hair flipping into my face.

He grabbed my ankles and dragged me toward him before he gripped my jeans and started to tug, not even bothering to unbutton them first. He chose brute force over inconvenience and continued to tug, taking my thong with it because my clothing was skintight.

He got my bottoms to the backs of my knees then bit me right on the ass.

I released a gasp mixed with a quiet scream.

He bit my other cheek before he tugged again.

I let out another scream, louder this time because he bit me harder.

He yanked off my shoes then got my jeans and thong off before he spread my cheeks with his hands and kissed my pussy, his nose in my ass, sucking with the same force as when he'd bit me, making my body twitch and writhe from the unexpected pleasure.

"Tell me you're on the pill." He stood up and dropped his pants and boxers.

I looked over my shoulder, my eyes immediately on his forklift of a dick. I stared and stared, seeing the veins run from base to tip, the fat dick that would have to ram its way inside me if it wanted to fill me. "IUD." It was all I could get out at the moment, seeing the sexiest man ever at the foot of my bed, with a dick that could support an Olympic medal around its base.

"Good." His knees hit the bed, and he smacked me with his palm, hit me hard on the right ass cheek.

I let out a gasp from the hit. "Fuck."

He smacked me again, harder this time.

"God..."

He grabbed both of my wrists and pinned them against my lower back before he smacked the other ass cheek, the hardest strike of the three.

"Fuck."

"Look at those handprints." He kept his grip on my wrists and kissed my cheeks, dragging his tongue over the inflamed skin in apology. His mouth returned to the place where I throbbed most, and he kissed me there, still aggressive but purposeful, like he really wanted to make me wet for his entrance.

I breathed through the pleasure, fighting the grip he had on my wrists every few seconds, my spine arched to accommodate the way he held me. The sting on my cheeks mixed with the bliss between my legs, and the result was a perfect mix of pain and pleasure. My senses were on fire, and now the sensation of every touch was magnified tenfold.

He released my wrists and moved over me, the bottom of his chest against my back and his dick right in the crack of my ass. He ground against me, his mouth coming close to my ear. "I'm gonna fuck this pussy—and I'm gonna come inside this pussy." He continued to grind against me, pushing my pelvis into the bed and providing a bit of friction against my clit. He gave me a couple seconds to resist his intentions.

I didn't want to resist them. "Are you clean?"

"Always."

He didn't ask me if I was clean before he put it in, before he pushed his massive head through my entrance and sank deep inside, breathing a sigh of satisfaction when he felt how slick I was, how slick I'd become the first moment I saw him.

I moaned when I felt him push deep, create so much pressure on my channel, invade my lands like they'd never been claimed by anyone else. "Oh god." I felt him grip the hair at the back of my neck and tug hard, forcing my chin up and my eyes on him.

He started to grind against me, supporting his muscular body with his legs and a single arm, thrusting deep inside me, treating me like prey captured by an apex predator, pushing me into the bed with his weight.

I closed my eyes and bit my lower lip because it was so damn good. I'd never been fucked like this, like an escort with a fee worth a Maserati, a price this man would pay in the blink of an eye because he wanted to fuck me so bad.

"Look at me."

My eyes snapped open and locked on his.

He ground into me directly, making my clit push and drag against the bed, knowing how to do it just right.

I moaned and whimpered, feeling the heat grow between my legs more and more, feeling the dam of tears break behind my eyes before they emerged.

He released a moan from deep in his throat, the sexiest sound. His hand loosened from my hair, and he gripped my neck instead, right below my jawline. "Spread your cheeks for me."

I was so deep in the haze that I didn't think twice about it. I gripped my cheeks and pulled them far apart.

He gave an appreciative moan then stuck his thumb in my mouth.

I instinctively sucked it, feeling his big dick do amazing things to me.

He pulled his hand away then slipped his thumb into my back entrance, pushing deep inside unexplored territory.

I tensed because I'd never felt anything like that before. Never had a man go for my rear. It was like the spanking of my cheeks, the novelty and discomfort highlighting the pleasure. In just a few seconds, I was panting and moaning, jumping to the finish line when there should have been some distance to the end.

And then I came, tears streaking down my cheeks, my breaths erratic and quick.

He pulled his thumb out of my ass and returned his mouth to my ear. "Fuck." His tone held so much satisfaction, like the sounds and feeling of me coming around him were foreplay for him, like he got off to a woman's pain as well as her pleasure.

I got swept up in the storm of euphoria, and my feet left the floor. A climax was a climax, but this one told me they weren't all equal. This one told me that they could reach the glass ceiling and shatter it.

He stilled and continued to breathe against my ear.

I'd assumed he finished when I finished, but his dick was still rock hard inside me. He dipped his head and kissed my shoulder and then my neck, lavishing me with his masculine kisses.

Then he pulled his dick out of me—and spanked me hard.

I winced at the pain, feeling another handprint on my cheek.

He grabbed me and rolled me onto my back before he made himself at home between my thighs. He tugged me and bent me the way he wanted me before he pushed inside me again, sliding in easier this time because he was already lubed up with my arousal. He sank in then gripped me by the throat and squeezed.

I could still breathe, but barely.

I finally touched him, felt just how hard that chest was, touched the ink all over his skin, the heat that burned from his flesh. I gripped his wrist and squeezed as he fucked me into the pillows, as his strong physique tightened and shifted, his physicality so unrealistic it seemed fake.

He moved his thumb up my throat to the corner of my mouth. He squeezed again before he let me go, before his hand found a home in my messy hair.

I cupped the side of his face as I planted my other hand on his chest, feeling his heartbeat through his mass. "Fuck, Bastien..." This man was a complete stranger, but I moaned his name like he was my long-term lover, like I'd loved him for a lifetime, had already given him sons and daughters. I should feel guilty for being with someone new while technically still being married, but I felt nothing of the sort. I just enjoyed it—thoroughly.

He pounded me into the bed, one arm pinned behind my knee, while the other remained deep in my hair, his blue eyes gripping tight like I belonged to him. "Here it comes, sweetheart." Up until that point, he'd thrust hard and fast without changing his pace, not needing to edge himself so many times like Adrien did. But Bastien slowed it down, moaning between the thrusts. "You want it?"

"Yes." I cupped his cheek and breathed with him, lost in the clouds of lust, connected to this man so deeply it was hard to believe I'd met him just a few hours ago. One-night stands were never this satisfying. It usually took a couple times before the sex got good. But right off the bat, this chemistry was electrifying. "Come inside me."

"Beg." His fingers fisted my hair, and he pinned me in place, his eyes turning sharp and hard, his dick still pounding into me, his balls hitting the bottom of my ass.

I widened my legs farther and gripped his ass, tugging him into me. "Please..." I didn't know myself. I was on fire, lost in the spontaneity and the ferocious lust that burned between us, letting this man fuck me exactly how he wanted...and I didn't even know his last name.

"Fuck." He moaned under his breath then pounded into me hard, giving me all of his dick over and over, making me wince from the size but ignoring the signs of pain on my face. "Here it comes." He moved his lips to my ear, and his pumps slowed as his breaths turned erratic. He gave his final pumps and filled me, came inside me like I was more than a one-night stand.

I'd never done anything so irresponsible in my life, but I wanted him to the exclusion of everything else. I couldn't explain it, but I wanted all of him, every piece of him, inside me. When I told Adrien, he would have no interest in making the marriage work, and I knew that was the best for both of us.

Bastien came to a halt, his fair skin tinted red with arousal and exertion. He held himself over me, and I expected him to pull out and begin his awkward departure, but he stayed buried inside me, still hard even though his come coated his base. "I've got a lot more bullets in this gun."

Chapter 2

Fleur

I woke up the next morning to the cold.

The curtains were drawn closed even though I hadn't touched them, and without opening my eyes, I knew Bastien wasn't there. He might have left after I'd fallen asleep, or maybe he'd woken up with the dawn and slipped out.

Unlike most men, he was honest about his intentions, so his absence wouldn't sting. Of course it would be disappointing, because let's face it, I would never have sex like that again in my life.

I would never see a man as beautiful ever again.

Would never see Bastien again. I'd be lying if I said that didn't bother me...a little bit.

When I opened my eyes, I looked at the intensity of the light coming through the line between the curtains and tried to gauge the time. I felt a slight headache behind my eyes, probably from lying in one spot for so long. As I expected, Bastien was gone.

I sat up in bed and rubbed the sleep from my eyes before I reached for my phone, but I realized I had no idea where it'd gone. Was probably still in the bottom of my purse and somewhere in the hallway.

I groaned as I got out of bed and wandered the hallway, but my shoes and purse were nowhere to be found.

Bastien looked like a bad boy, but a thief? I doubted that. I stepped into the kitchen and found my heels together on the floor near the counter and my purse on the round dining table. My phone was also there, next to the glass vase I'd found at the market, of a woman's ass. The second I'd seen it, I'd known I needed it in my apartment now that I was a single girl.

When I tapped the screen, my phone lit up and showed the time—high noon.

There were also messages piled up that had come in throughout the morning. I opened the message box, but instead of looking at the messages at the top, I noticed texts from the name Bastien buried farther below, delivered around six in the morning.

I opened the message box. ***Had a meeting early this morning. Didn't want you to think I was a dick.***

The last thing I'd expected was his name programmed in my phone, along with a message, especially since I had a passcode lock. He'd somehow bypassed that even though he didn't strike me as a tech genius.

I didn't know what to say. He wouldn't have put his name in my phone if he didn't want to be in contact with me, but I made my peace with the fact that it was a one-time thing. I suspected Bastien was the kind of man that didn't just break hearts, but did so irrevocably. I'd already had my heart broken once, and I wasn't looking to break it again when it hadn't healed from the first injury.

So, I moved on to the other messages and went about my day.

I was at work when he walked inside.

Not he, as in Bastien, but he, as in my soon-to-be ex-husband, Adrien.

He took a seat at the bar and looked at me with his classic pissed-off expression.

I stared him down with the most irritation I could muster. "Why are you here?"

He continued to stare at me, a tint to his face.

"Are you going to order something or...?" I didn't have time for this immature bullshit. There were other people sitting at the bar. Even though it was a weeknight, it was a packed house.

"You had someone at your apartment last night."

I stilled at the statement and felt the anger seep in. "You're watching me?"

"Making sure you're safe—"

"I'm not doing this here." I wanted to raise my voice but couldn't. "You're a fucking prick, you know that?" I walked away and moved on to somebody else in the hope he would leave. I served drinks and kept my eyes on my customers and my hands, and after thirty minutes of ignoring him, he finally left.

But I knew he would be waiting in my apartment when I walked inside.

When I entered the apartment, the lights were already on. I walked into the main room with the dining table and tossed my purse on it, not looking at Adrien even though I spotted his frame in the corner of my eye. "Who the fuck do you think you are?" I turned to look at him head on.

His eyes held unspent rage. "Your husband."

"Not by choice," I snapped. "What part of 'give me space' do you not understand?"

"Space to fuck around?" He raised his voice, like this truly burned holes through his skin.

"I'm not obligated to tell you a damn thing because I'm not your wife anymore. But unlike you, I'm a decent and honest person who's as transparent as glass, so I was going to tell you. Paying your men to watch me twenty-four seven is completely unnecessary."

His face started to blotch red, his anger having no escape except through his skin.

"I met someone I liked—and I fucked him." If Adrien hadn't bombarded me at work or admitted he was having his men tail me, I would have been a lot more delicate about it, but I was too pissed off to cushion his feelings. "And it was gooooood."

He started to tremble, like his head was about to explode from the audacity of my words. He dragged his hand down his face like he needed to move in some way so he wouldn't pick up a chair and throw it at me. He turned around and started to pace, too much rage coursing through his body to tolerate.

"So good, I'm glad you cheated on me—let me put it that way."

He pivoted back in my direction, his eyes so vicious it seemed like he might hurt me. "I know what you're doing, and it's not going to work."

"What am I doing?"

"An eye for an eye. I get it."

I released a weak laugh because it was ridiculous. "No, Adrien. I don't keep receipts or settle scores like you do. I fucked him because I don't want to be in this marriage anymore, and I'm ready to move on with my life. So let's file those divorce papers and go our separate ways."

"Last time we spoke, you said you would think about it."

"And then I met this sexy-as-fuck man and realized I don't need to settle for your bullshit. All I asked was for you not to stick your dick in other people, something you promised when we married, but apparently that was too fucking hard."

He rubbed his hand over his jawline again, knowing this marriage was exploding in his face right now. "It was a mistake."

"And this guy wasn't a mistake. I knew exactly what I was doing when I did it. And you can't fool me, Adrien. You knew exactly what you were doing, too. Just fucking own up to it. Maybe then I would have been willing to work it out with you, but the fact that I had to hear about it from her, of all people..."

"I said I was sorry—"

"Sorry that you got caught. Big fucking difference."

"If it was a one-time thing that I regretted and would never repeat, why would I hurt you by telling you that?"

"It's called honor. It's called honesty. It's called integrity. And more importantly, it's called respect. You did not respect me when you fucked her. You did not respect me when you chose to hide it from me. You spared me the pain of the truth by lying about it, but you hurt me in far more ways by keeping it a secret. I'm done with this marriage, Adrien. Grant me the divorce so we can move on with our lives."

He stared at me as he breathed hard, watching his world come apart in ash and fire.

"Adrien, you're handsome and rich as fuck. You can be single and fuck all of Paris if you want. You don't need a wife."

"As hard as this is for you to believe, I married you because I loved you." He said it with complete seriousness, suppressing his anger so it wouldn't escape in his tone. "I still love you. I can replace you with beautiful women that I'll forget, but I genuinely, truly want to be married to you."

It was the first time I felt my anger pause. I crossed my arms over my chest and let out a quiet sigh.

"But once you found out, you took off. We haven't had an opportunity to really talk because all you've done is run. I won't pretend that this...fling...doesn't bother me. Doesn't rip me apart on the inside. But I suppose it is fair...so I can let it go." With every word, I sensed his massive restraint, like it made him sick just to say these things. "I still want to work this out. I still want you to come home."

My chin drifted down, my arms still tight across my chest, my eyes on the floor.

"Fleur."

My eyes stayed down. "You say there was no one else, but I'm not sure I can believe you. That's the problem." I lifted my eyes and looked at him again.

"There was no one else."

"Is there actually no one else, or is there just no way for me to find out?"

He released a quiet sigh in frustration.

"If there's no trust, I don't see how this is going to work. There's shattered glass everywhere, and I'm going to keep stepping on it."

His eyebrows furrowed like he didn't understand what that meant.

"The answer is no, Adrien."

44

"You won't even try—"

"Because I don't trust you. And no amount of marriage counseling is going to fix that. I'm always going to wonder if there were others. I'm always going to wonder if I've become that dumbass woman who actually believes her husband is a good man when he's lying to her face. I don't want to be a fool, Adrien."

"I think you're a bigger fool for throwing this away—"

"You're the one who threw this away. I won't let you turn this on me."

He stared at me for a long time, anger and frustration burning in his gaze. "What I said still stands. Try with me—or there will be no divorce."

"Whoa..." I shook my head. "If you wanted me this bad, then why did you fuck someone else? Where was this fight then? Where was this obsession? Is this actually about love or propriety? Or is it about wanting what you can't have? Is it because you're a child who can't stand it when you don't get your way?"

The defeat was in his gaze, the frustration that had nowhere to go but deeper inside. "I love you, Fleur. From the first moment I saw you. I refuse to let you go, not just because I don't believe in divorce, but because you're the love of my life. I'm willing to do anything and everything to make this relationship work. It's that simple. So, there will be no divorce, not until I see you try, not until I see some real effort to make this work. If we try and give it our all and you still can't trust me, then so be it."

"How many times do I have to say it? I don't want to try."

His defeated look morphed into something else, an expression that was subtly deranged. "Don't fight me on this."

"You know fight is my middle name."

His eyes contained the same razor's edge. "You can continue to submit the paperwork to the courts, but it'll be rejected every time. And if you try to have a relationship with someone else, I'll make sure they know you're married—*to me.*" The threat was never stated, but it was unmistakable. He was connected to a lot of people in his line of work, because whoever could afford such invaluable pieces of art and had no objection to owning a piece of history that belonged to the people clearly didn't have a conscience. And they were capable of far worse than purchasing stolen artwork.

"Then I guess I'll pick my next man wisely."

Chapter 3

Bastien

It was almost midnight.

I sat in the council chamber, upon a throne that Louis XIII had sat upon himself, in Luxembourg Palace, a sprawling estate claimed by the French Republic in the late seventeen hundreds. It was the place where the Senate gathered, where the president of the Senate lived in one of the pavilions on the property.

My knife was on the pedestal in front of me, the hilt carved into the seal of the Republic.

I sat there and waited, Antoine and Luca on my left and Gabriel and Mael on my right, me in the dead center.

One of my hands stepped into the room. "They await your judgment, Butcher."

I gave a slight nod, ushering them to come inside.

Their wrists zip-tied behind their backs, they were dragged into the council room, a place where King Louis had once held court. The windowsills were made of gold, the ceiling was seventy feet high, painted champagne pink with a chandelier in the center.

Two of them didn't fight, but the one in the middle did, as if there was any chance of escape.

The hands dropped them in the center, in front of the pedestal that held my knife.

They were already bloody from the beating they had received from my servants, their eyes bruised shut, their noses broken. One of them lay with his head to the floor, knowing it was over. The one in the center was ornery, staring at me like I was the one on trial.

I stared back at them, my cheek propped against my closed knuckles, looking at them like the vermin that they were. "On Tuesday evening, you attempted to rob Silencio with machetes—and threatened a girl behind the counter." The crime was petty compared to most criminals I dealt with, but no one was above the law. "You know the law—*Homines ex codice*."

"I didn't hurt her." The one in the center had a face now that his mask had been stripped away. He was a young man, probably someone who just needed to get by and had decided to steal from the rich.

"You threatened her with a knife—and called her a bitch."

"It wasn't personal—"

"You know the law."

He let out a scream. "I didn't touch her!"

"You cased the area before you hit it. You could have picked a different place, picked a bar run by a man, but you chose that one." I said it simply, casting judgment the way I had a hundred times, taking no pride or regret in my position. "The first French Emperor of the Senate hereby condemns you to death."

He pushed to his feet and attempted to flee, but one of the hands shoved him to the floor again. "I didn't touch her. I didn't rape her. I didn't traffic her. You're telling me I deserve the same punishment for greater crimes?"

I rose to my feet and approached the pedestal that held the old knife, a weapon that Napoleon had carried while he was emperor and during his exile on Elba.

"It's not fair!" He tried to get to his feet again to rush me, but the hand kicked him to the floor.

"You didn't just pick the wrong bar—*but the wrong girl.*" I gripped the knife and brushed my thumb over the handle before I looked to my fellow Emperors. "Is this punishment just? Or perhaps I'm unable to see clearly..."

Gabriel looked at the others, and a silent conversation seemed to pass between them. "If she was untouched, then perhaps the carve is more appropriate. Everyone who gazes upon them will recognize your mark. They will know that justice was served."

I considered his words before I slowly turned back to the C-level criminals at my feet. One of them was shaking uncontrollably. Wouldn't be surprised if he pissed his pants. These amateurs would ordinarily be beneath my attention. "Then they shall be carved." I nodded to the hands.

They moved to the three men on the floor and forced them upright, their hands yanked back to expose their faces.

I went for the one in the center, my thumb pressed against the hilt as the tip of the knife rested against his cheek.

His panting turned hysterical, and he hyperventilated right before me, knowing, like so many others, he would bear my mark and all would know he'd been punished by my hand. "It wasn't personal."

"I know," I said as I pushed the knife through his skin. "And neither is this."

I walked into the office of the pavilion at the palace, a great mahogany desk on the thick rug. Outside were the gardens, statues and carved bushes for the public to admire during their tours of the grounds. Most of the people were foreigners who would never understand our politics, no matter how many tours they booked.

Even our citizens didn't understand it.

Raphael Boucher sat behind the desk, the President of the Senate, the next in line for the presidency if President Martin were to become incapacitated. I took a seat in front of his desk as he finished up his phone call, a lit cigar between his digits, his wrist relaxed. He finally hung up and shoved that cigar into his mouth.

"Thought you were trying to quit."

He waved off the comment and smashed the cigar into the glass ashtray.

"Don't worry," I said with a smirk. "I'm not a snitch."

"The chief of police says a couple more girls have been taken." He stared me down as if this was entirely my fault, as if I was the one who had kidnapped them and shoved them in the trunk of a car.

"I'm working on it."

"Are you? Because I hear you're convicting a couple kids who tried to rob a bar."

"That was a personal matter."

He sat back in his chair and crossed his arms over his chest. "Bastien, we've got to put a stop to this. Cafés and restaurants are hurting because women aren't going out late anymore, and people are already pissed about the change in the pension system. Tourism is down because women are afraid to travel here—"

"You think I give a shit about any of that?" I snapped. "Tourism can be damned. I hate Americans as it is."

Raphael was a middle-aged man with short hair sprinkled with gray. He was thin and in shape, looking like an American businessman in his blue suit. He served the president of France and ran the Senate and the National Assembly—as well as the French Emperors—a secret society within the Senate that did all the dirty work so no one else had to. We weren't a group of vigilantes who wanted to punish crime. We wanted to run it—by our rules. We maintained crime, kept it healthy, and protected the innocent. Without us, the French Republic wouldn't have the most romantic city in the world.

"I'll handle it, Raphael."

"You said that six months ago."

I gave him a cold stare. "You want me to keep every criminal in this city in line. And you want me to capture the largest trafficker France has ever known at the same time. I know everyone worth knowing, and no one is saying shit about Godric. That says something...or the lack thereof does."

Raphael had just put out his cigar, but he grabbed another from his drawer and lit up right in his office, in the place where royalty had once sat. "Figure it out, Bastien."

I arrived at the private estate outside of Paris, armed guards behind the gate like they always expected trouble. I checked in with the guy in charge, and they radioed in my presence to the man of the house—Fender.

I sat in the car for a while as I waited for an answer, unsure if he would agree to see me without warning when we barely knew each other. It was at least ten minutes before the gates opened and they allowed me through.

I'd never waited for anything, but I waited for Fender because he was the best lead that I had.

The valet took my car, and the butler escorted me into the study, a place that smelled like cigar smoke because the scent had been absorbed by every piece of furniture and the curtains for decades.

I sat there, a copy of *The Count of Monte Cristo* on the coffee table next to a small vase of pink roses. The house was quiet like no one was there, but the place was three stories and probably full of staff.

A moment later, Fender walked inside in jeans and a long-sleeved shirt, his pissed-off expression reserved for me. He was a man in his forties, on the precipice of fifty, but he was still built like a brick shithouse, a man who lifted every morning without exception, who let his hair sprinkle with a hint of gray because he didn't give a damn to cover it.

He faced me on the other side of the coffee table, sizing me up with those coffee-colored eyes. "If this isn't important, I'll shoot you between the eyes."

He was deadly serious, and I liked that. "Fair enough."

He dropped onto the couch, arms on his knees, his palms together.

I sat across from him, the doors to his study open but the house quiet. "I spoke to Magnus the other day, but that was a dead end."

"He is a dead end." He was still dead serious.

"I'm sure you've heard women have been disappearing from Paris."

"I don't watch the news because I don't give a shit about anything outside my world. I keep tabs on my wife and children, and the rest can burn for all I care." His hostile eyes stared me down like bullets from a gun. "You wasted your time coming here."

"You operated the most expansive trafficking scheme in Paris fifteen years ago."

"Yes—*fifteen years ago*. And if the Butcher thinks he's gonna carve my flesh off the bone, I'd like to see him try." His hostility burned even hotter, like he'd jump across the table and strangle me right there on the couch.

"Statute of limitations," I said. "You're pardoned."

He still looked pissed off as hell. "I have nothing to offer you, Bastien."

"You must know someone I can ask."

"Fifteen years is a long time. Most of the people I knew are probably dead. Bartholomew from the Chasseurs settled down and moved to Tuscany. I don't know where Benton and Bleu ended up. Some LSD freaks took over the camp a decade ago, but I think they're all dead now."

I nodded in understanding. "Magnus said more of the same."

"Then you wasted your time—and my time—coming here."

"Are you always this hostile?"

His eyebrows rose slightly at the audacity of my question.

"President Martin may be the president of the Republic —but I'm the Emperor of France. Under my rule, *Homines ex codice* applies, which is in your best interest as a father and a husband. Crime is regulated, just the way our food and health care are regulated by the laws that govern this land—and I'm the one in charge of it. If you want your daughter to live in a place where she can walk the streets alone at night, where your wife can shop alone without fear of being in the wrong place at the wrong time, then you should help me in whatever way you can."

He cocked his head slightly as he looked at me, and slowly the hostility drained from his expression the way water drained from soil. Several beats passed, and his stare remained locked hard on my face. "I'll see what I can do."

It'd been a week since I'd walked into Silencio and met Fleur. I'd made it clear I wasn't a one-woman kind of guy, so I doubted she'd expected me to be there when she woke up, but I still felt obligated to explain my absence.

But I guessed the gesture meant nothing to her because she didn't text me back.

That was a first.

My driver pulled up to the bar, and I hopped out. It was midnight, just a few hours from closing, and a couple was outside on the sidewalk enjoying their cigarettes. When I looked through the window, I saw her standing at the bar and making a drink, an old-fashioned for the guy sitting at the very end.

I walked inside and saw that the tables were full of people having a late-night drink even though it was a weekday. But the bar itself was mostly empty because no one wanted to sit on a stool for hours on end, and they chose to gather at a table with a leather armchair.

She wore a tight long-sleeve black shirt, a deep V in the front to show the tops of her perky tits. A necklace sat in the center, a single pendant in rose gold. The details were too faint for me to read. The last time I'd seen her, her long hair had been straight and almost to her waist, but now, it was curled and shiny. Her makeup was dark, a smoky eye look that reminded me of a sexy cat, exactly the kind of shit I was into.

I took a seat on a stool, choosing the side where no one else was seated.

She didn't notice me right away, doing her nightly cleanup since it was slow.

I wasn't sure if I was impatient for a drink or her attention. "Want to make me a drink, sweetheart?"

She didn't turn at my voice, but she stiffened like she knew exactly who it belonged to. She folded up the towel she'd been using and turned to me. "The usual?" She recovered from the shock in just a second, and now she had the kind of confidence that implied she'd known I was there the entire time. She was quick on her feet, just the way she'd been when that idiot had come at her with a machete, having far too much pride to admit she'd been caught off guard.

"Sure."

She made me a drink, a double scotch on the rocks, and placed it on the counter in front of me. "Didn't expect to see you in here."

"Didn't expect you to ignore my texts."

"I didn't ignore them. Just didn't have anything to say."

I took a drink as I stared at her, wondering if she'd been thinking about me as much as I'd been thinking about her. Beautiful women were a dime a dozen, but this woman had something special. I wasn't sure if it was the I-don't-give-a-fuck attitude, the sass, or just her incredible tits—or all of the above.

"You said you had a meeting. Where do you work?"

I didn't answer the question, not wanting my reply to be overheard by anyone who may be listening.

She knew I ignored her, but she didn't repeat the question or pry into my silence. She worked on her cleanup in front of me, pouring out glasses and tossing old limes for the drinks. When her hair fell in her face, she would move it across one shoulder and expose one side of her neck, and I remembered how she'd tasted when I kissed her.

I remembered how her pussy tasted too. "Did you tell him?"

She smirked slightly, her eyes down on her work. "Yes."

"And did it fix your problem?"

She lifted her gaze and looked at me, her head slightly cocked like her barrel was full of sass and ready to blow. "No. In fact, it made it worse."

I felt the smile try to move into my jawline. "Damn, that backfired."

"Yep."

"Sorry about that." I continued to smirk. "Well, not really..."

She chuckled, her cheeks reddening slightly.

"Maybe a second round would do the trick."

"I don't know," she said with a sigh. "He said some shit, and I don't think he was bluffing."

"What kind of shit?" I asked, turning serious. "Did he threaten to hurt you?" Because I would cut his eyes out of his head and force him to eat both.

"No. I can say a lot of bad things about Adrien, but not that," she said. "But I know he wouldn't hesitate to hurt whoever I'm with." She continued her work and avoided my gaze, like she assumed this information would bring our fling to a standstill.

"In that case, your place or mine?"

"Bastien, I don't want to get you mixed up in my soap opera—"

"Your place or mine, sweetheart?" I took a drink.

She stopped what she was doing. "He's watching my place. That was how he figured out you were there."

"So you didn't tell him."

"He beat me to the punch. But trust me, my fist was clenched." She walked off to help the patron who came to the bar. Her back was to me, so I stared at her ass as she made the drink for the old man and charged it to his tab.

I lifted my eyes when she returned to me.

"Subtle."

My fingers rested against my mouth, and I felt my lips

rise in a smile. "Wondering if those handprints are still there."

"They aren't," she said. "I checked..."

I remembered her tight ass in my grip, the flesh between my teeth, the velvet softness of her slick pussy, the way her hair clung to her neck when she got sweaty, how she begged me to come inside her like I was more than some guy she met in a bar. "I'm happy to give you a new set, sweetheart. All you have to do is ask."

"Last time I wanted something, you made me beg for it."

I was a man with a permanent scowl, but she made it impossible not to smile. If this was a volley without an end in sight, she was a worthy opponent. "And I'll make you beg again—and again."

———

She closed up the bar, and we stepped onto the curb. She wore a long coat and wrapped it around herself like she intended to walk home through the mist at two in the morning. "Are we walking?"

I texted my driver and slipped the phone back into my pocket. "No."

The SUV pulled up a moment later, and I opened the back door so she could climb inside.

She hesitated, her carefree attitude suddenly gone when she saw a driver appear at my beck and call. But then she climbed into the back, and I got into the other seat. We were on the road, driving through the empty, wet streets to my residence in the 7th arrondissement, a three-story palace on the Seine next to the Eiffel Tower. It was close to Luxembourg Palace, where I spent a great deal of my time.

She was silent on the drive, her gaze focused out the window.

A short while later, the car pulled up to the front of my home, a building I owned entirely. It used to house several apartments, but I'd turned it into my private residence. It had its own gardens, an interior courtyard, its own secure entrance that couldn't be accessed from the street, and it contained fifteen bedrooms and twelve bathrooms. I'd bought the property for a total of one hundred million, and the renovation had cost an additional twenty million. If she was acquainted with money, she would understand exactly how much of it I had.

When we pulled through the gate, her eyes widened slightly then quickly returned to normal, like she knew but was too classy to react outwardly.

We entered through the double doors and came into the foyer, fresh flowers in vases, artwork on the walls, chairs and sofas that no one had sat on since I'd moved in. Hallways branched off to different places, like the drawing room, the study, the grand dining room, the kitchens. All of those amenities were downstairs where the staff stayed.

I guided her to the stairs and went to the second and then the third floor. My primary bedroom had double doors, taking up the back part of the top floor, a space where an entire apartment had sat before I'd renovated the whole building.

When we walked inside, the curtains to the windows were still parted, showing the Eiffel Tower lit up like a Christmas tree, the bank on the other side of the Seine illuminated by the lampposts.

In her heavy coat, she stared at the Eiffel Tower as if she'd never seen it before, her eyes reflecting the lights that shimmered from the base to the top.

I watched her appreciate something the rest of the French had forgotten, a historic landmark with eternal beauty. I got lost in my stare, savoring the way the light brought a distinct glow to her face. She didn't inspect my chambers or care about their luxury. All she cared about was the view.

"I can't see it from my apartment," she explained. "Just the rotating searchlight when it hits the other buildings."

"Where was your old place?"

"The 8th arrondissement—near the Four Seasons."

She'd gone from a life of luxury to a one-bedroom apartment near a mall, but she didn't complain about it. She chose the hard life over the easy one, and I respected the hell out of her for it.

I came up behind her and removed the heavy coat from her body, tossing it over the back of a chair before I pulled her against me, one arm locking in front of her shoulders while the other slipped underneath her shirt and rose up to her chest. I slipped my fingers under her bra, and I took one of her plump tits in my grasp. I squeezed it harder, felt her chest rise with the deep breath she took. I gripped the other one as I locked her against me, listening to her breathe and feeling her lean into me, her breaths starting off quiet before they rose in intensity.

My hand left north and headed south, traveling over her flat stomach, her pierced belly button, and inside the front of her jeans. I slipped my fingers under the soft fabric of her panties, felt the smooth skin over her pelvic bone, and I felt her inhale a sharp breath just because I touched her most erogenous spot.

I glided my fingers over it before I pressed into it hard, making her repeat the breath and the gasp. She grabbed on to the arm that was across her collarbone, and her nails dug into the flesh as she arched and pressed her back into my chest.

I continued to play with her clit as I tightened my grip over her shoulders, my lips pressed to her ear. "Look at the tower." I rubbed her throbbing nub as I stared at the side of her face, seeing her eyes shut as she continued to writhe, her feet digging into the floor and pushing, squirming.

Her eyes opened and reflected the brilliant lights. Her breaths took on volume, becoming labored in their intensity, matching the way her body ground and rocked against me, her legs shaking as her feet continued to dig into the rug.

My grip kept her in place against me like a bird trapped in a cage, and I played with her little pussy, plunged a finger into her river before I smeared it over the nub that was on fire. I chose force over a gentle caress, and that made her whimper louder, made her breathe hard like she was getting fucked in the ass.

I knew she was almost there, the tide rising higher and almost covering the entire beach. With a little more, she would convulse against me, her nails drawing blood. When I had her where I wanted her, I pressed my lips near her ear. "Beg."

She released a groan when she felt my fingers slide away from her aching channel.

"Beg me to fuck you." I slipped my hand underneath her shirt again and squeezed her tit, her arousal wet on my fingertips, coating her nipple as I pinched it. The trail of moisture over her tummy glowed in the light.

So deep in the haze, she didn't even try to fight it. She turned into my chest and lifted my shirt over my head before she locked her mouth on mine, rising on her tiptoes and tugging my neck down so she could reach my lips. She dug her fingers into my hair, and she hiked her leg up my hip like she wanted me to pick her up. "Fuck me."

I lifted her into me, our mouths finally level, her mouth ravenous like a hungry wolf.

"Please, Bastien." She cupped my cheek, and she kissed me like I meant the world to her, like a wife happy for her husband to come home after the war, like a woman who'd only loved one man all her life. "Fuck me, Bastien." She said the words against my lips, barely pausing our kiss to speak. "Hard."

I carried her to the bed and rolled on top of her.

"*Please.*" Her anxious fingers moved for my jeans like there was a gun to her head.

"Jesus." I grabbed the back of her jeans and started to tug them off.

"Hurry," she said, out of breath. She tugged my jeans and boxers down so my dick came free. "Come on."

I growled in impatience, but fuck, I'd never wanted to fuck a woman more. I had been the one teasing her, but now she'd flipped the tables on me and I was none the wiser. I tugged her shoes and socks off before I got the jeans the rest of the way.

"Hurry up," she said in the sexiest voice. "I can't take this." She writhed on the bed, kicking her feet to get everything free of her skin, a distinct glistening between her legs because she oozed from my touch. She pulled off her shirt and got the bra free, her beautiful hair a mess because she moved in such a rush.

My dick was exposed to the cold air, but it twitched with desperation. I finally kicked off my shoes and got my jeans the rest of the way off.

"I said hurry."

"Fuck, woman." I moved on top of her, and her thighs immediately opened to let me in. The insides of her knees gripped my torso and squeezed, and my dick found her slickness like it was locked on a target. I pushed through her entrance and sank in a single motion, flooded with enough arousal to fill the entire Seine. "Jesus..." I dug my fingers into her hair and fisted it.

She cupped my face and breathed against my lips, writhing and whimpering, her other hand hooked over the back of my shoulders. She released the deepest sigh of pleasure, packed with emotion, like my dick was the only thing that would bring her satisfaction. Then she said my name in the sexiest way, as a desperate sigh, the kind that made bumps appear on my arms and tightened my spine. "Bastien..."

I sucked in a breath and closed my eyes briefly, because damn, how was I supposed to last like this? When this fiery woman begged me, whispered my name over and over, dug her nails into my flesh like she'd never let me go. Every time I thrust, I wanted to come undone, this pussy too tight and slick for my hungry dick to handle. I always wore a condom during my rendezvous with regulars and my hookups with strangers, but for some reason, I skipped the protection with her. The sight of her pussy turned me into a hungry bear that wanted her honey all for myself. "Sweetheart, I can't last like this..."

She grabbed on to my ass and tugged me hard into her. "I want to feel you come inside me."

"Fuck." My ass clenched as I thrust, my body taking over and sliding through the softest velvet. My dick burrowed inside her over and over, her slickness spilling over and seeping into the sheets beneath us.

She cupped my face and then traced the tattoo of the knife at my jawline. "I want to watch you come inside me." Her lustful eyes looked into mine with a sex-drunk haze, fully enveloped in the moment with me, like we were more than two people who'd met in a bar. Her other hand tugged on my ass, wanting all of my dick even though it hurt sometimes.

I felt my body burn so hot I was about to shed my skin like a snake. My dick hardened just a little bit more before the end and felt like a metal rod in her silky softness. I was covered in her arousal, a pool of it underneath my balls from tapping against her ass. My breaths turned shaky, and I lost feeling in my fingertips because my core took all the focus.

She continued to trace my face with her fingers, her smoky eyes so confident and sexed up, gazing at me like I was a god who walked the earth.

I felt the heat spread to my face, felt the color burn my cheeks. My thrusts turned erratic, and then I shoved myself deep as I released, giving a loud growl as I grabbed on to her neck and squeezed.

She clutched my wrist, and she moaned with me, taking my come alongside her own climax. Her hips convulsed against me and matched my pumps, both of our bodies giving in to the animalistic pleasure we felt.

I filled her little pussy with the first round of the night, and I stayed hard like I was ready for the second. I hooked my arm behind one of her knees, and I folded her underneath me before I pounded into her like a jackhammer against concrete, fucking her good and hard, one hand on her throat to muffle her moans.

She stroked my hard jawline then dragged her hands down the ink over my neck and palmed my chest, touching me like she could feel the fire against her fingertips. Her lips were parted and her tongue was slightly visible, as she panted through the pleasure between her legs and the pain from my grip around her throat.

She guided my face to her mouth so she could kiss me, and that was when I released my grip on her throat. "Fuck, you're so hot." She said it between kisses, melting into me like we were both streams of lava from the same volcano merging together.

I knew what I had to offer, but women rarely complimented me, choosing to play it cool and feigning indifference as if that would capture my attention more than honesty. But Fleur wore her heart on her sleeve, told me her thoughts when she had them, didn't play it cool at all —and that was fucking refreshing.

But I was the one with the spectacular view, her tits beneath me, her toned legs open to accommodate me, her little pussy full of my big dick. A lot of beautiful women had been on this very pillow on nights identical to this, but she was different from the others. Her ferocity, her desperation, the way she didn't give a damn what anyone thought of her—including me.

I'd drifted off at some point. I lay beside her, the Eiffel Tower still visible through the window, and the cocktail of good sex had lulled me into sleep. But then I stirred when I felt her leave the bed and follow the breadcrumb trail of her belongings on the floor. She picked up her shoes and found her jeans and panties, but then she stopped to look out the window at the Eiffel Tower, appreciating it like a tourist who'd come to the City of Lights in search of whatever she was looking for.

She lingered for at least thirty seconds before she carried her belongings to the other room to get dressed.

I could lie there and pretend not to notice her departure. There would be no awkward conversation about the next time we would see each other. It was exactly what I wanted—usually.

But not this time.

I left the bed and pulled on my boxers before I stepped into the other room.

She'd just gotten her bra on when she gave a flinch. "I didn't mean to wake you."

"Is there something wrong with the mattress?"

"What?" she asked, clearly tired, her makeup a mess from the sweat.

I snatched the shirt out of her hand and tossed it on the table. "You don't have to run out of here."

"Oh, it's okay," she said as she grabbed the shirt again. "I've got a busy day tomorrow."

"Doing what?" I called her bluff.

She looked at me again, her eyes shifting back and forth between mine like she didn't understand the question.

"Stay." I grabbed the shirt again. "I'm not asking." I moved closer to her, sliding my hand into her hair as I kissed her, felt soft lips that reminded me of juicy plums in summer. My thumb touched the side of her mouth, the skin that was softer than the flesh of a nectarine.

Her response was immediate, catching my mouth on instinct and kissing me like we'd just walked into the house. All the stiffness in her body faded when I touched her, her hands cupped my face, and she kissed me back like she was instantly swept away by the chemistry that burned white-hot between us.

I lifted her into me and carried her with a single arm because she weighed nothing. I laid her on the bed and moved over her, like this was the start of the night rather than the end of it. I pulled down her panties for the second time, and I slid inside her, squeezed by her slick tightness, by the deposits of seed I'd already left earlier in the evening.

She moaned like it was the first time rather than the fifth or the sixth, clinging to me like she'd lose her way if she let go. "Bastien..."

When I woke up a second time, she was still there.

Good.

I tapped the screen of my phone on the nightstand to see the time. It was twelve-thirty. I looked at her, seeing her dead asleep with the sheets to her shoulder, the white pillows covered in marks from her makeup, her hair a mess from the way I'd used the strands like reins to a horse.

I texted Gerard, my head of staff. *Prepare breakfast for two on the balcony.*

His response was immediate. *Of course, sir.*

I set the phone on the nightstand then moved to the double doors that sectioned off the bedroom from the rest of my chambers. I closed them, so when Gerard delivered breakfast, he wouldn't be able to see the two of us in bed.

She didn't stir.

I left the bed, put on my sweatpants, tossed a shirt on the bed for her to wear when she woke up, and stepped into the other room where my laptop was on the desk in the sitting room. I opened it and did some work, checked some emails.

Thirty minutes later, Gerard let himself inside, and without acknowledging me to remain quiet, he wheeled the cart onto the patio over the Seine and set up breakfast, putting down a white tablecloth before placing the covered dishes on the table. When he was finished, he opened all the curtains so the sunlight came into the room. It was a clear day, a sunny morning for Paris.

Once he was gone, the doors to the bedroom opened. She came out, her face clean like she'd washed off in my bathroom. She'd gotten the hint about the t-shirt I'd left on the bed because she wore it, the black shirt fitting her like a dress. Her hair was brushed like she helped herself to my comb, not that I minded.

She moved to where her clothes sat, folded into a neat pile by Gerard. Then she looked out the window and stared at the table set up on the balcony, the sun reflecting off the murky water of the Seine.

"Hungry?" I shut the laptop and came around the desk.

Her eyes immediately shifted to me, looking right at my chest and abs as if I didn't have a face. Her gaze dropped farther down, looking at the top of the sweatpants low on my hips. She drew a slow breath before her eyes flicked up to me. "I love a hot guy in sweatpants."

She spoke her mind with no regard for my opinion about it, and that was damn refreshing. She didn't put on a production for me, didn't try to be quiet and mysterious, didn't try to entrap me by playing hard to get or saying whatever I wanted to hear. She was genuine, down-to-earth, exactly who she was.

And anyone who was brave enough to be themselves was the bravest of all.

With the corner of my mouth raised in a smile, I walked up to her and bent my neck down to kiss her, my hand gripping one of her cheeks underneath my shirt. It was so plump and meaty in my grasp, and I grabbed her hard enough to leave a mark.

Her lips trembled against me like it hurt but she still liked it.

I opened the double doors to the balcony and pulled out the chair for her before I sat down. It was an unusually warm afternoon in the city when the sun was out like this, when the wind was blocked by the building so the air was stagnant. I poured the coffee then removed the lid over my plate to eat.

Her coffee was more milk than coffee, and my coffee was black.

She removed the silver platters that covered her dishes, and her eyes widened in pleasant surprise. "Blueberry pancakes, a savory crepe, and a side of bacon and toast... Wow. Good sex, and now this? Guess karma is a real thing." She drenched her pancakes in maple syrup and took a bite, closing her eyes as she savored it. "Damn, this is good shit." She moved on to her crepe and took a couple bites of that, nodding as she savored the taste in her mouth. "Fuck yeah."

I watched her, unable to stop the smirk from entering my lips.

When she felt my stare, she tensed. "Sorry...haven't had breakfast like this in a while."

I imagined she hadn't eaten out much since she'd gotten her own apartment because it was too expensive. She'd probably had staff at her marital home, so this was a taste of her old life, a life she'd walked away from because her principles were more important.

I mostly drank my coffee and took a couple bites of my breakfast. It wasn't until later in the day that my appetite kicked in. I usually started my day with a session in my personal gym, so that was probably why my stomach hadn't woken up yet.

She drank her coffee then looked out over the river, seeing the people on the other bank having a picnic. When the weather was nice like this, people went out to enjoy the sunshine. Notre-Dame was visible in the distance, the cranes sticking out because it hadn't been rebuilt since the fire that had caused so much damage. She enjoyed the view for a long time, taking a break from her food to savor the sight.

I watched her in the silence, the distant sound of voices barely reaching us from the road below. An ambulance went by and the sirens were loud, but then it was gone in a couple seconds and it was back to the quiet.

"I love this city." She seemed to say it more to herself than to me, like a thought meant for herself had accidentally been expressed.

"What do you love about it?"

She turned at the question, her green eyes locking on mine. "Everything."

"I want specifics."

She looked into her coffee as she composed her response in her head. "That our modern lives are intertwined with the past." She turned to the bridge in the distance. "Napoleon's mark endures for centuries." The big N carved into the stone was visible, even at this distance, his mark on all different kinds of landmarks, especially the Seine, so anyone who entered Paris by boat would still know the emperor. "The building we are in now has probably been here since the sixteenth century. I think that's really special, that you can see what Paris used to be even when you walk through the streets and the cars. The way the city is lit up so bright at night, that you can walk anywhere and never get swallowed by the dark. The way we're obsessed with food the way Americans are obsessed with money. It's the only place where people want to walk in the rain. The place of great artists and writers and poets...a place full of such creativity. I don't care how expensive this city is, how small my apartment is. I'm not leaving for the suburbs because it's cheaper. I'll hook on the street if I have to."

"If it ever comes to that, I'd be happy to pay for your services."

She smiled slightly, a blush moving into her fair cheeks, her eyes on the Seine. "Do what you love and never work a day in your life, right?" Her eyes found mine, and the second we made contact, her smile started to fade.

"You think I'm joking." I'd be happy to make her my private whore, put her up in a beautiful apartment where her only concern would be to fuck me—and only me. Her husband had made the greatest mistake of his life sticking his dick in someone else, because now I was going to stick my dick in her every night.

She broke contact and drank her coffee. The silence trickled by as she did her best to act like that part of the conversation had never happened. "I'm not sure what direction my life is going. I don't have an education and only have a little work experience. Most people are passionate about something. But to be honest, I'm not passionate about anything."

"All I've seen from you is passion."

Her eyes came back to me.

"You're passionate about this city. You're passionate about food. And you're very passionate in bed."

Her eyes dropped down to her coffee like she didn't want to face the truth, that she was a vixen in bed who clawed my back until I bled. It seemed to bring her a heavy sense of shame.

"Why does that bother you?"

"What?"

"The way you fuck me."

"It doesn't bother me," she said quietly. "I just...feel guilty about it."

"Why the fuck would you feel guilty about that?" Her husband had ended their marriage the moment he betrayed her. She owed him nothing—not a damn thing.

"I know it's stupid—"

"It is stupid."

She looked at me again. "We've only been separated for a month. I'm not one to keep receipts or hold grudges, so jumping into bed with someone else isn't really me." She wore heavy makeup whenever I saw her, but she looked just as beautiful without it, especially in the afternoon light. The fact that she didn't care if I saw her without makeup was sexy. "But the moment I saw you walk into that bar...I wanted you."

I felt a tightness all over my body, a flush of desire unlike anything I'd ever experienced. I'd already had her, and by now, I should be bored of her, but the desire only got worse. So much worse.

Her stare remained on mine, confident enough in herself to pull off such a statement. She never breached the territory of arrogance, never even coming close to that line. "I'm sure I'll figure it out. I always do."

Chapter 4

Fleur

Bastien's driver took me home.

He pulled up to the building and let me out, and then I took the long walk up the stairs to my apartment. If Adrien was still watching me, and he probably was, he would know that I had been gone all night.

Which meant he was in my apartment right now, waiting to bulldoze me.

I got the key into the lock and stepped inside. When I walked to the dining table where I normally put my stuff because it was such a small apartment, I saw him on the couch, looking mad as hell. "This really needs to stop—"

"We are still married." He got to his feet, the volume of the choice making the glass shake. He was the maddest he'd been since the day I'd met him, his face red like a tomato. "You think I'm out fucking around?" He raised his left hand, showing the wedding ring he claimed he never removed.

"You were fucking around when we were married, so—"

"Enough of this." His hand tightened into a fist at his chest, doing his best to control the rage that enveloped him. "We are married, Fleur. Husband and wife. Till death do us part."

"Our marriage ended the second you fucked someone else, Adrien. Just because the courts recognize us as legally married doesn't mean our hearts are married. You can keep blocking the judge from granting the divorce, but that doesn't mean a damn thing. We are done."

"You said you would think about it—"

"I said I needed space. Don't twist my words around."

He stepped closer to me. "You said you would think about it until this asshole showed up. Who is he?"

Like I would answer.

"Tell me his fucking name."

"No." I did not need two guys fighting over me like lions.

"You haven't been out of the house for a month and you're already moving on, but I'm the unfaithful one?"

"Adrien—"

"We are married."

"You can keep saying that, but it doesn't make it true," I snapped. "It's a goddamn piece of paper. Doesn't mean a damn thing."

"You think I won't kill this guy?" he barked. "Because I fucking will."

"When Cecilia told me you fucked her, do you think I went apeshit and threatened to kill her and all this macho bullshit? No. I said thank you for letting me know and walked away like a normal person. You act like this guy is responsible for our divorce, when I left you before I met him. You act like he's the problem when you fucking someone else was the problem."

He paused for a moment and dragged his hands down his face, like that was all he could do to stop himself from throwing a chair across the room. "I've been miserable these last four weeks. Fucking miserable. And you don't seem all that upset to me."

"You don't know the half of it." The nights I cried in my apartment alone, the raindrops pelting the windowpane and matching the drops on my cheeks, the days when I didn't eat anything at all. The days when I couldn't breathe at all. "You have no idea how much you hurt me because I won't fucking show it. I won't give you the satisfaction."

"Satisfaction?" he asked incredulously. "I hate myself for what I did. Would do anything to take it back. Everything that made this marriage work is still here. You and I are both here. Just come home and make this work with me."

I crossed my arms over my chest and stepped away, still smelling Bastien all over me, feeling his hands on my cheek and my neck. "I believe you're sorry, Adrien. I believe you would take it back. But that's not enough for me, not when I feel this way."

"People make mistakes, Fleur. I'm not perfect and neither are you."

"I know," I said simply. "But this is one mistake I don't want my husband to make." I wanted a happily ever after. I wanted to be the only woman in his life, to know where I stood in his heart at all times. To not care when he was out late at night because I knew he was faithful to me.

Adrien started to pace slowly, his dark wedding ring still on his hand, his handsome face forlorn in defeat. He stopped at the window and dragged his fingers across his jawline. I expected him to say something else, but he didn't. He just stared out the window I'd stared out so many times, and then he walked out.

Days passed, and the numbness in my veins continued to spread. Rejecting Adrien over and over had taken its toll.

Even though I'd moved out because of his treason, I had been in shock for weeks. I'd sat by the window and cried my heart out. Sometimes I'd wondered if Cecilia was lying because she had an ulterior motive, but Adrien confirmed his infidelity, so it was true. The last person I'd expected to hurt me had hurt me the most.

And then I moved into the next stage of grief—*anger*.

It was easier to be angry than to actually feel the sting of his deceit. It was easier to hate him than to think about how good it felt for him to fuck her and think he got away with it. It was easier to be angry than to accept that my marriage had only lasted three years before it went to shit. It was easier to be pissed as hell than to admit that I really loved him...and that was why it hurt so much.

I was on the couch watching the rain hit the windows when my phone vibrated with a text. Adrien hadn't contacted me since he'd left, so I suspected it was him, unable to maintain the silence a moment longer.

But I checked the screen—and it was Bastien.

You haven't been at work.

The rush of passion I felt for him was dulled by my sadness. **I've been off.** That was a lie. I'd called in sick because I didn't want to wait on people with a fake smile plastered to my face. The burglary had had no effect on my well-being, but this divorce had stripped me to the bone.

You okay, sweetheart?

How did he know? How could he possibly read my misery through a text? *Why do you ask that?*

Because I can tell you aren't yourself.

I stared at his message over and over, unable to understand how he could read me so well. How he seemed to know me so thoroughly when he was still a stranger. When he was just a man who kept my bed warm and chased away the loneliness. I never responded to the message, unsure how to do so. Most of the friends I had were friends with Adrien, and while they thought he was an asshole for what he did, they all agreed I should give him another chance because he loved me. So I stood on the mound of my principles alone.

Let's get a drink.

I'm not in the mood...but thank you. I set my phone aside then looked at the rain again, watched it hit the window and streak down. There was a heaviness to my heart, an anchor that would make it sink to the bottom of the river and remain there forever. I hadn't felt this bad since the day I'd moved out of the house. Adrien had let me go, but he must have suspected it was temporary at the time.

Thirty minutes later, there was a quiet knock on the door.

My eyes turned to the hallway, unsure who would come to my door when I was on the top floor and Adrien just let himself inside whenever he felt like. It might be a solicitor, so I stayed on the couch and waited for them to go away.

Then the door opened, and Bastien appeared in my apartment.

I was in shock, so I just stared, unable to believe this gorgeous man had just let himself into my apartment like he had the key. He had a paper bag with him, and he placed it on the dining table without explanation. He was in sweatpants, sneakers, and a long-sleeved shirt, looking like a regular guy rather than someone who was insanely rich.

There were a lot of rich people in Paris. It was one of the most expensive cities in the world, so it was full of people who made their millions in all sorts of ways. Bastien was young, so I should be surprised by his hundred-million-euro house by the Seine, but somehow, I wasn't.

He took a seat beside me on the couch, his arm resting over the back, leaving a foot of space between us. Then he stared at me, not seeming to care that I looked like shit after sitting on that couch for days, watching the world pass me by like I was no longer a part of it.

He continued to stare.

I stared back, and with every passing second, I felt better. Like the light from his eyes somehow healed me. I didn't ask why he was there, didn't ask how he'd gotten into the apartment, didn't ask all the normal questions I would have asked someone else. When Adrien broke in to my apartment, it made me so angry. But with Bastien, I didn't care.

He hadn't blinked since he sat down, looking at me with such intensity it seemed like he might kiss me, even though I knew he wouldn't.

I cleared my throat. "What's in the bag?"

"Those pancakes you like."

My eyes softened at the unexpected gesture, a gesture that a man like him seemed incapable of making. "You didn't have to do that."

"I know." His fingers rested on the back of the couch, close enough they could touch my hair if they wanted, but they stayed put. "We can talk about it or not talk about it. I'm here either way."

"I don't understand..." I remembered our first conversation in that bar, remembered looking into those startling blue eyes like it had just happened. The way his voice had sounded over the quiet noise of the piano, his confident aura. "You aren't a nice guy, but you're being awfully nice to me."

He didn't say anything to that, just continued to stare at me like I'd never said anything.

I didn't dig deeper. "He hurt me first, but I still hate hurting him."

He watched me in silence.

"I'm not the one who cheated, but somehow I feel like the bad guy."

He didn't give advice or cast judgment. Just sat there and listened.

"He kept asking who you are."

"Tell him."

"You don't need the drama in your life."

"I'll read him a chapter from *Manhood*," he said. "He obviously hasn't read it."

"I'm really afraid he might try to kill you."

He released a quiet chuckle. "That'd be fun to watch."

I pulled my knees to my chest, circling my arms around them. "Everyone in our life is telling me to give him another chance. My friends are saying it was a mistake and he loves me. He keeps showing up at my apartment and fighting for me."

His blue eyes turned serious as he stared at me, steady like a cliff that stood still when the waves broke against the stone.

"You're thinking about everyone else when you should be thinking about yourself. What do you want, sweetheart?"

My eyes flicked away, realizing he was right, that I was more concerned with everyone else. "What you said about trust being like broken glass, it's really stuck with me. No matter how many times I sweep, I still step on shards that I missed."

His eyes burned into my cheek, steady and true.

"What do you think?" I turned back to him.

He smirked. "You can't trust my opinion, not when it's so biased."

"Why is it biased?" I asked.

He cocked his head slightly, his eyebrows furrowing in a form of confusion. He propped his closed knuckles against his temple as he continued to look at me, giving me a long and hard stare. "Because I want you."

My eyes immediately dropped to shut out the sincerity of his stare. He'd told me he wasn't a one-woman kind of guy, that he stuck his dick in lots of places so he wouldn't settle down. I assumed that was still true, even now. But I felt doubts.

"Look at me."

My eyes lifted to his again.

"I already gave my opinion on this. All a man has in this world is his word. If he doesn't have that, then he doesn't have shit. Your husband can look you in the eye and say it'll never happen again, but because his word is worthless, it falls on deaf ears. But if you love him and want to give it another try, then you need to give him the opportunity to earn back that trust. And there's no shame in that—if that's what you want."

I spoke to him like a friend even though I hardly knew him. Poured my heart out to him like we'd known each other forever. I'd never had another connection like that. When Adrien and I had started our relationship, it wasn't nearly as natural. "What if this were you? What if your wife slept with someone and said it was a mistake?"

He inhaled a slow breath before he let it out, as if he'd just taken a puff of an invisible cigar. "That's a hard scenario to imagine."

"Because you'll never marry?"

"Because I can't see my woman doing that. Can't imagine her seeking love and affection elsewhere when I'd already given her everything."

"I gave him everything. The bedroom wasn't dead. We were very happy when all of this happened, which makes it even more painful."

"I didn't mean to imply that you didn't," he said gently. "Trust me, it's hard for me to imagine a man preferring another woman over you. No amount of wine can impair you to that degree."

That made me feel better—and made me feel worse. "You didn't answer the question. What would you do...if that did happen?"

He took another breath as he considered it, his eyes drifting off elsewhere as he thought. "I've never loved a woman so I can't definitively respond to the situation, but I imagine if I did...it would be hard to let her go."

"So, you think I should give my marriage another chance?"

"Not what I'm saying at all," he said. "The situations are incomparable—and hypothetical. I see that you're searching for an epiphany, something that will help you understand which route to take, so let me tell you this..."

I stilled, knowing whatever he would say would be profound.

"You're too fucking beautiful for this bullshit. Because if you were mine—" He shut his mouth immediately but kept his eyes locked on mine, like he wished he could take back what he'd said, but it was too late. "You wouldn't have to make this decision in the first place."

Chapter 5

Bastien

She lay in my arms for a while until she fell asleep, her head against my shoulder, the rain continuing to splatter against the windows. I looked out into the night and just enjoyed the sound, savoring the peace that hardly ever visited me.

I scooped her into my arms and put her in bed before I covered her with the sheets. She didn't wake up, just like a child that was tucked in for the night. I turned off the lights and walked out, making my way down to the bottom floor and out through the double doors.

A man in a raincoat leaned up against the wall of the café across the road. Another one was seated on the outdoor patio of Nelson's, the restaurant on the other side of the walkway. I didn't wear a coat and I embraced the rain, loving the way it felt against the back of my neck, the way it smelled, the way it made the asphalt glisten, something only a real Parisian could understand.

I walked up to the man in Nelson's, and he worked so hard not to be suspicious of me that I immediately became suspicious of him. Even when I was right at his table, he refused to acknowledge me, his black coffee sitting there untouched.

"Bastien Dupont."

He had no other choice but to look at me.

"That's my name."

We sat in the parlor, cigar smoke hanging in the air and blanketing the elegant room in a haze of fumes. With one elbow on the armrest, I puffed on that cigar and let the taste of black licorice float on my tongue before it released as a stream of smoke from my mouth.

Luca lounged in the chair, tilting his head back as he aimed his cannon of smoke toward the ceiling. "They'll never pass it. Damage is done at this point."

"Nothing is set in stone, especially in politics."

"You think the Senate will overturn it?"

I kept the cigar in the corner of my mouth. "I really don't know—and I really don't care."

"Doesn't apply to us, now does it?"

"No." I rested the cigar between my fingertips and took a drink.

"Is there a problem, Bastien?" Luca asked, tapping his fingers against the cigar to make the ash fall into the tray. "You seem pissed off."

"I'm always pissed off."

"More than usual, then."

I hadn't spoken to Fleur since I'd left her apartment. Wasn't sure what she'd decided, if she wanted to give her marriage another try...or continue to fuck around with me. I did my best to stay out of it and be objective, but it was hard to keep my mouth shut. "I'm sleeping with this woman, but she's married."

Luca was about to take another drag of his cigar, but my words made him forget about it. "That was not what I expected you to say." He sat up and put out the cigar in the communal ashtray on the table. "What does it matter if she's married?"

"Because she might take him back."

"So, they aren't married?"

"Separated. He cheated on her and she left him, and he's been trying to get her back ever since."

"So, she used you for revenge sex?"

"I don't think so." Whatever we had, it was real.

Luca stared at me for a long time, waiting for me to say something more so this story would make sense. "I'm not following, man. You had your fun. Now it's time for her to go back to her husband. Everybody wins."

"But I don't want her to go back to him."

"Why?"

"Because she deserves better than that shit." I grabbed the glass from the side table and took a drink. "And she knows it too."

"Then maybe she won't take him back."

"Maybe." But I hadn't heard from her. I didn't want to pressure her or persuade her in any way. I'd given my information to one of the guys who was watching the apartment, but her pussy of a husband hadn't contacted me. Once he figured out who I was, he probably realized we weren't in the same league.

"You like her or something?"

After we fucked on that first night, I didn't expect to see her again. All I had to do was walk out, and that would have been the end of it. But something made me put my number in her phone, something I'd never done before. "Yeah...I do."

Once Luca realized this conversation was serious, he stopped the bullshit and straightened. Now, he didn't say anything at all, waiting for me to explain the situation.

"I don't know, man. I can't explain it." I could explain it, the way we came together and set the room on fire, the way we turned into Adam and Eve, destined and created for each other. But that would require details I refused to share. "But yeah, I like her. And whether she takes him back or she doesn't...it's shit timing."

He remained quiet, his unblinking stare on me. "Yeah, it is. Does she know who you are?"

"No."

"Then she doesn't know you at all."

"I guess you could say that." She'd asked me how I earned a living once, but because we were in public, I never answered. She didn't know anything about me personally, other than the fact that I was rich, something she never asked about.

I loved that she didn't ask.

Gerard stepped into the drawing room. "Sir, Adrien Laurent is here to see you."

"Speak of the devil..." I turned to Luca. "That's him."

"Her husband?" he asked with his eyebrows raised.

"Yep."

"I'll back you up."

"I don't need backup, Luca." I put out the cigar and rose to my feet.

"He's got a lot of balls coming here," Luca said. "Are you sure—"

"I'm fine." I gestured to the door. "I'll talk to you later."

"Alright." He let Gerard escort him out of the room. He might have passed Adrien on the way.

I stood there and waited for Adrien to join me, surprised he had the spine to face me, unless he didn't understand who I was. Well, if he didn't, he was about to. I stood in my sweatpants and t-shirt, not afraid to do business in casual attire. My real uniform was my knife anyway.

Footsteps sounded, and then he rounded the corner—in trousers and a blazer like a fucking pussy. He had short brown hair with matching eyes, tall and lean, not packed with muscle the way I was. In hand-to-hand combat, he'd be dead.

He stilled as he sized me up, looking me over as his opponent. He was outmatched if we were in the ring with boxing gloves—and he was outmatched as a lover too. I might have a pretty face, but I was packed and tatted.

The standoff lasted for a solid minute, Adrien coming to terms with the fact that I was the man bedding his wife.

Soon-to-be ex-wife, I hoped.

He finally took a breath like he needed to steel his nerves before he approached me. He didn't fire off with threats and bullshit right off the bat, so he was smarter than I'd assumed. "Of all the men in Paris, she had to pick you."

"I think she has great taste."

An explosion of rage flashed across his eyes, but he didn't act on it. "She has no idea who you are."

"Separation of church and state."

He came closer, the table between us. "I think she'd feel much differently if she had all the facts."

"I don't know. She seems pretty tough to me." Handled those handprints beautifully. Didn't mind my thumb up her ass. Didn't scream when some asshole came at her with a machete. The girl had a backbone—and I liked that.

"Tell her, or I will."

I smirked. "Is that what your mistress said to you?"

His eyes narrowed once again. "I'm sure someone like you doesn't give a shit about marriage—"

"Quite the contrary, actually. Assholes like you are the ones who shit all over it."

He bypassed what I said. "I know I fucked up. I admit that. But that doesn't mean I don't love her. I know we could work it out if you would just go the fuck away."

I couldn't wipe the smirk off my face, not when it pissed him off so much.

"She said she would consider a reconciliation—and then you showed up."

"I tend to do that."

"You think this is a joke?" he snapped.

"You thought it was a joke first when you pissed all over your wedding vows. Or should I say *came* all over your wedding vows?"

"Fuck you, Butcher."

This was the part where I bragged about all the fucking I did with his wife, but I had too much respect for her to say a word. I wouldn't rub my conquest in his face, not when I had to drag her name through the mud to accomplish that.

"She doesn't mean shit to you—and I love her. So stay the fuck out of my relationship, alright? You claim to be the Justice of Paris, but you're bedding another man's wife when he's trying to put that marriage back together. Fucking hypocritical."

"You would have been divorced if you hadn't stopped her paperwork—to be fair."

With a burning anger in his eyes, he clenched his jaw. "Are you going to step off or not?"

I barely knew the woman. I'd had good sex, some that I paid for and others that were free, but with her, it was different. Couldn't explain it. But her situation was complicated, and the timing just wasn't right. "I'll bow out. But if she comes to me, she's fair game."

The restaurant had closed to the public, but I walked inside like I owned the place—because I did. All the tables were crammed together, but they were empty of plates and already wiped down for the night.

Manuel stood at the bar, and he greeted me with a nod before he headed to the back. The kitchen staff was still working after the rush they'd had. From what I'd been told, reservations started a month out.

Guess the place was good.

There was a lone table in the middle, the only one that was easily accessible and not pushed up against others. I made myself a drink at the bar then sat down. The street outside was a one-way road, and sometimes people passed the window. It was a cold evening, but I got warm as I walked, so I hardly ever wore a jacket, not unless it snowed.

I sat there and drank my wine, listening to the chef yell at the staff because he yelled at everyone. He was a good cook, so I let him run his kitchen however the fuck he wanted. *L'Ami Jean* was an old establishment, one of the oldest restaurants in the city, even before the Second World War. I bought it because I wanted to keep it exactly the same forever. History and legacy were important to me—and not just because the blood of the nobility ran in my veins.

Minutes later, my guest joined me, wearing a pea coat like a goddamn pussy. He barely looked at me before he took a seat across from me, dark hair and eyes, an ugly scar over his left eyebrow where a hook had dug into his flesh years ago. He looked at Manuel and ordered him around like he was his own employee. "Make me a drink, son."

Manuel looked at me.

I nodded.

Manuel poured him a glass of wine before he set it on the table.

He took a sip before he finally looked at me. "Butcher."

"Darius." I crossed my arms over my chest. "Hope you have good news."

"I do. We resolved our shipping disputes and have prepared the payment."

"Good."

He pulled out his phone, did some typing, and then passed the screen to me.

I checked the funds before I hit send and slid it back.

He did it again, calculated the total, and slid it across the table toward me.

I eyed it, making sure the details of the sender were encrypted before I hit send and handed it back.

Darius dropped the phone into his pocket. "I appreciate your patience."

"I appreciate you doing your job. Less work for me—and my knife."

He smirked as he reached into his jacket and grabbed a cigar before he lit up.

I'd had enough for the day, so I didn't join him.

"Lemme ask you something, Butcher."

"I suspected something was coming down the pipeline." Most of these transactions didn't happen in person. In the digital age and in my special line of business, physical goods were unnecessary.

"You could make a lot more if you cut ties with the Fifth Republic. A lot more."

"I'm aware."

"Then why?" he asked. "You could work for me."

"I don't work for anyone, Darius. And I don't work for the Fifth Republic either."

"Then you could work *with* me," he said. "Imagine what we could do. Imagine the margins if we bent the rules—"

"Some say rules are meant to be broken, but not mine. As long as I live and breathe, they will remain. There's no reason the criminal enterprises that flourish in this city can't continue to thrive with order. What I've done has created an economy that benefits everyone, from the criminals, to the Republic, and to the people."

He leaned back in his chair, trying to smile through my words despite the annoyance that built in his eyes.

"Maybe you could earn more under different circumstances. But isn't it better to operate lawfully?"

His only answer was a shrug. "We'll have to agree to disagree, Butcher."

I continued to sit there, arms across my chest, the workers still scrubbing the pans clean in the back.

He continued to smoke his cigar.

"Tell me about Godric."

He smirked before he released the smoke from his mouth. "What makes you think I speak to him?"

"You have the same politics."

His smirk remained, and it was accompanied by a slight nod. "Quit while you're ahead, Butcher. You know what happens to snitches..."

They were mauled in the street, on the way to the car after a nice meal at their favorite restaurant, in broad daylight in the midst of afternoon traffic. Stabbed with knives from every direction, they would have thirty knife wounds before they hit the street—and the attackers would blend into the crowd. There were more codes than mine.

"So, you do know him?"

"If you wanted to play poker, you should have brought the cards."

I smirked slightly at the joke. "I'll find him."

"Good luck with that."

"And there will be hell to pay when I do."

"I'm sure." He reached into his pocket and pulled out a folded manila envelope before he plopped it on the table. "Here's everything you asked for."

I opened it and pulled out the contents, a full report with photos, phone records, and text messages. I'd barely glanced at it and was overwhelmed by the mound of evidence. "That son of a bitch..."

"You better sharpen your knife."

Chapter 6

Fleur

It'd been a couple days since Bastien had come by the apartment. I'd eaten the pancakes when he'd left, and they were just as good as the first time I'd had them on the terrace of his home along the Seine. But I hadn't heard from him since, and I hadn't heard from Adrien either. It was the first time I'd heard nothing from either of them.

I went back to work at the bar, and Bastien didn't show up for a drink. Adrien didn't stop by to harass me either. My life became quiet and unremarkable. That forced me to experience the pain head on, to think about what I wanted to do.

Try to save my marriage...or move on.

I was in my apartment when Adrien texted me. **Can we talk?**

I should appreciate how much space he'd given me this last week, even though I shouldn't have to appreciate anything from him, not after what he'd done. **Sure.**

I'll be there in a minute.

That meant he was outside my apartment, at one of the cafés downstairs, or sitting in the back of his driver's car. Just when I thought I had some space, I realized he'd been suffocating me this entire time.

He walked inside a moment later, wearing jeans and a sweater because a chill had swept across the city.

I was on the green couch, my knees to my chest, wearing leggings and a long-sleeved sweater, my loungewear. I wore no makeup because I didn't have the energy to care about my appearance at the moment.

He sat in the armchair, arms on his thighs, looking at me with trepidation. "I can apologize to you again and again, however many times you need to hear it. It was a lapse in judgment, a momentary mistake, something I'll regret forever. But we still love each other—and I think this marriage is worth fighting for."

My stomach was clenched like a fist, the pain and the rage mixing into a bowl of acid.

"Could we just try?"

My eyes flicked to the window behind him.

"Fleur—"

"What constitutes trying?"

"Whatever you're willing to do. You could move back in and have your own bedroom—"

"I don't want to go back there."

"Then you can stay here, and we could do marriage counseling a couple times a week. Perhaps a professional will help us heal the wounds and help you trust me again." He sat at the edge of his seat, like he wanted to fling himself forward and grab me hard. His eyes flicked back and forth between mine as he waited for my answer.

I wouldn't be this depressed if I didn't care about Adrien. I would be able to get out of bed if I didn't care. But I was defeated, and the time apart had only made me feel worse. Did that mean I was love-sick? But I also had a deeply passionate relationship with a man I hardly knew, so what did that mean? That I was delirious? That I was just seeking comfort anywhere I could? I didn't have the answer to any of those questions. "Okay..."

He continued to stare at me, his expression slightly blank as if he didn't realize what I'd said. "Okay? Did you just say okay?"

I nodded.

The biggest smile moved over his face, a glow in his eyes that was brighter than Christmas morning. "That—that makes me really happy. Thank you so much—"

"This doesn't mean we're getting back together. It just means...I'm willing to start somewhere."

Chapter 7

Bastien

Since he'd paid me an unexpected visit at my home, I decided to do the same to him.

My driver pulled up to the gates, and I stepped out to speak with the guard. After a brief conversation, he let me pass into the courtyard. It was a nice building, the luxury understated and tasteful. It was an expensive piece of property, but it was nowhere near as expensive as mine.

I was even more impressed that Fleur had left it all behind to start over on her own.

Fuck, she was so hot.

There was a fountain in the center, potted plants and hydrangeas spread around. It looked like a spot for lunch, when the sun was directly overhead and the wind was blocked by three walls.

One of his staff approached me. "I'll take you inside, sir."

"He can meet me here. It'll only take a moment." I wouldn't set foot into the house of my enemy. Not when I despised him so deeply.

The man gave a nod then stepped into the home.

I waited, the courtyard well lit despite the late hour. It was almost midnight, so the city was finally starting to doze off.

Adrien joined me minutes later, dressed in his lame blazer again. His eyes shifted back and forth as he looked at me, like I was there to kill him. "What's the meaning of this?"

"Don't worry, I'm not gonna kill you—at least not today." I held up the envelope then threw it right at his face. "Tell her, or I will."

He caught the envelope before it hit the ground, but he kept his eyes on me the entire time. "Tell her what—"

"Would you like me to kill you today?" I marched up to him, making him take a step back toward the fountain in the center. "Fucking tell her, or I will. And trust me, you don't want it to come from me."

Chapter 8

Fleur

I sat in the armchair in the office, the blinds behind the desk closed. A clock sat on one of the dressers, the ticking of it loud in the quiet space. The marriage counselor was already there, a woman in her sixties, someone who had enough life experience to handle a delicate situation like this. We talked about the weather for a while, and I looked at the small vase in the corner of her desk, fresh roses there like she'd picked them from her own garden.

Adrien was late, which was ironic, considering he was punctual for every appointment. He actually got me here, and he hadn't even shown up.

A minute later, he walked inside and hurried to his seat. "I'm so sorry I'm late." He turned to me, apologizing to me more than the therapist. His hand reached for mine on my lap. "I'm so glad you're here—"

My hand immediately withdrew, like his touch was the plague.

He stilled at my actions then retracted his hand.

A pair of blue eyes flashed across my mind, eyes that were so pretty but so hard at the same time, that could drill past my vacant stare and see the depth of who I was below. His hand had gripped my throat, had marked my ass where he'd struck me, had cupped my face in the gentlest way.

I looked away from Adrien and swallowed.

Linda was the name of our marriage counselor, and she had just witnessed our first interaction. "Trust has been broken. There is also deep-seated resentment. A lot for us to work through." She looked at us with a nonjudgmental gaze, like she saw this sort of thing all the time, a woman working past her husband's infidelity.

"I never thought I'd be sitting here." I stared at the roses, pink with dark shading along the edges, like they were wild rather than the curated ones from the professional gardens outside of Paris. They looked like they grew in a pot on someone's terrace, surviving the rain and living for the spots of sunshine between the clouds.

Linda looked at me. "Would you care to share more, Fleur?"

I shook my head. "We were happy. At least, I thought we were."

Adrien cut in. "We were happy—"

"Let her speak," Linda said. "It's clear how difficult this is for her."

I swallowed before I continued. "I thought I had a husband who loved me, truly loved me, and I know all women think their men will never cheat, but I actually believed it. I've done everything I can to be a good wife. I'm the same size as the day he married me, I cook his favorite things, give him love and affection and make him feel worthy of my heart... But it didn't matter." I focused on those roses because they were the only things I could grab on to, but what I really wanted was a pair of blue eyes that burned with strength.

The images came to me again, the shadows in the corners of his bedroom, the lights from the Eiffel Tower as they shimmered and danced, the way he kissed me like he loved me one moment and threw me on the bed the next. I didn't know who I was when I was with him—but I liked her.

When it was clear I had nothing more to say, Linda turned to Adrien. "How does that make you feel, Adrien?"

He was quiet for a while, trying to find the right words. "It hurts me to know that Fleur is searching for the blame...when I'm the one who fucked up. She did nothing wrong. I was just a fucking idiot. There's no better explanation than that. The experience has shown me how much I love my wife, because I would do anything to take it back."

I didn't take my eyes off the roses.

You're too beautiful for this bullshit.

I felt his thumb in the corner of my mouth, felt his fingers tangle my hair with their grip, smelled him even when he wasn't in the room, felt the comfort of his protection like he was there that moment.

"How does that make you feel, Fleur?"

I didn't even know him.

Didn't know his last name.

I'd fucked him bareback, begged him to come inside me, dug my hands into his hair so he couldn't leave. From the first moment I saw him and dragons breathed fire in my belly, I'd known he'd leave a mark on me that was as permanent as a tattoo.

I didn't know him.

And I didn't know me when I was with him.

"Fleur?"

My eyes lifted because they'd sunk to the floor. "Sorry..."

"It's okay," Linda said. "This is difficult."

"How did you fuck her?" I lifted my chin and looked at him.

He stilled at the question, like he couldn't believe I asked that. "Fleur..."

"Did you throw her on the bed? Did you grab her by the hair? Did you come inside her?"

Adrien looked shocked by the questions. "I—I don't think the details matter."

"I'm just trying to understand," I said. "Because if it was the best sex of your life, then it would make sense."

"You're the best I've ever had, Fleur."

"Really?" I asked. "Because you aren't mine."

Even Linda's eyebrows lifted at that statement.

Because we had an audience, Adrien hid the anger he would normally show. He had to bottle it and swallow whatever he would have said.

I turned to Linda. "Did you pick those yourself?"

It took her a moment to understand that I referred to the roses on the corner of her desk. "I saw you admire those. Yes, I have a small garden on my terrace. Do you like to garden, Fleur?"

"No."

Linda grabbed the small vase in her hands and rose to her feet to bring it to me. "How about you keep this—" A bit of water swished over the top and streaked down the side of the vase and over her hand. It made the surface slippery, and the vase fumbled out of her hands and smashed to the floor, pieces of glass flying everywhere, mixed in the pool of water and rose petals. "Oh dear, I'm so clumsy."

Adrien immediately went to her aid. "Let me help you. Do you have a broom?"

"Yes, in the closet," Linda said.

I just sat there and stared at the broken glass. A piece had landed next to my shoe—and another clear across the room in the opposite corner.

Linda picked up the large pieces and set them on her desk while Adrien swept with the broom, getting most of the shards into the pan. They worked together, neither seeming to care that I didn't bother to get up and help.

When Adrien was finished, he dumped the glass into the garbage can. "I think I got it all."

My eyes went to the piece in the corner and then the one right by my shoe.

"I'm sorry about all of that," Linda said. "Sometimes I forget I'm not as quick as I used to be." She returned to her seat behind the desk.

Adrien smoothed out the front of his shirt and retook his seat.

The commotion died down, and it turned quiet once more.

My eyes remained on the glass in the corner, the piece that wouldn't be noticed for a while—until Linda stepped on it and heard it crunch under her shoe.

"Now, where were we?" Linda said.

My eyes finally left the glass, and I looked at the woman who'd barely gotten a chance to know us, whose work was done before I even walked in the door. "I want a divorce."

Linda stilled at my statement, and then her eyes flicked to Adrien.

He cleared his throat. "Fleur—"

"I want a divorce," I repeated.

"We're here," Adrien said. "Can we at least finish the session?"

"No."

He released a sigh. "Please. You said you would try."

"And I tried," I said calmly, knowing my heart was dead and no amount of drugs or paddles were going to restart it.

Linda looked at me. "May I ask what prompted such an abrupt change? Because you seemed receptive when you walked in the door."

I glanced at the glass in the corner again. "Because my trust is shattered, and there are too many pieces to put back together."

"We were there for less than ten minutes—"

"It's over."

He followed me into the apartment. "You said you would try."

"And I did try." I turned back around. "You know how hard it was for me to go down there? No one gets married expecting to get divorced, but I really thought we would last. I really thought we were different—like a freakin' idiot."

"We are different."

"No, we aren't. We're just another couple where the husband fucks around because he's rich and thinks his wife will just put up with it."

"It was one time."

"That's what you say..."

"Fleur—"

"I'm so fucking done with this." I threw up my hands in frustration. "I don't want to be married to you anymore, Adrien. I don't want to try. I just want to move on. Stop forcing me to do something I don't want to do. If you love me, you'll let me go. If you're the man you say you are, you won't use your resources to block my attempts to be free of you."

Adrien was rooted to the spot, looking cornered like I was the one who came at him. For the first time, he was speechless, out of ammo. "Why do I feel like *he* has something to do with this?"

I felt myself stiffen even when I didn't hear his name. He still had his grip on my throat, still had his thumb in the corner of my mouth. Our time together had been brief, but it left a lasting impression. "I haven't spoken to him in a week." He hadn't contacted me. That could mean he moved on with someone else or lost interest. Or he wanted to give me the space to figure this out—unlike Adrien, who was down my throat every other day.

"That didn't answer the question."

I held his stare and my silence, unsure what I would say even if I could speak freely.

"He's dangerous, Fleur. Trust me on that."

"You've hurt me far more than he ever could."

He stepped forward. "You don't understand." His eyes shifted back and forth between mine. "*He is death.*"

I didn't know what that meant, but bumps formed on my arms anyway.

"If you're looking for marriage and kids and security, he is not the answer."

"I'm not looking for anything right now, Adrien. I'm just trying to put myself back together. I'm just trying to get through tomorrow and the next day." I stepped away from him, feeling no connection to him whatsoever. "I've lost my friends, the family I thought I would have forever, I lost you..."

"You didn't lose me." His hand moved over his chest. "I'm still here."

"I lost you the moment you stuck your dick in someone else." I turned my back on him and faced the window, feeling the crackle in my chest and the ache in the back of my throat, the warning of impending tears. I hadn't cried in front of him because I was too proud to let someone know they hurt me, but now, I struggled to keep my emotions in check, struggled to keep it together even with my back turned. "Please just go...and don't come back."

Chapter 9

Fleur

A week passed—and I didn't hear from Adrien.

I hadn't tried to submit the divorce paperwork again. I was too afraid I would be met with another rejection. And then I would have to confront him and have the same conversation I'd had a hundred times already.

I continued to work at the bar even though I wanted to cry on my apartment floor, but I had bills to pay now. I needed food and electricity and all the other essentials that I'd taken for granted when I'd married into wealth. That meant I was required to show up for my shift, regardless of the state of my mental health.

It was a quiet night at the bar. Some of the tables had occupants, but no one sat at the stools at the counter. I had no one to wait on, which meant no tips, which meant a smaller paycheck. A lot of people assumed that people who worked in hospitality in France were paid a great salary without tips, but that really wasn't true. We'd come to ask for tips and gratuities on tabs because additional income was needed to survive in a city like this.

No one was around, so I pulled out my phone and opened our message box.

I read his last message. **Let's get a drink.**

I'd rejected the invitation, and he'd brought me pancakes instead, an awfully sweet thing for someone with a dangerous reputation to do. I didn't call off the reconciliation with Adrien because I wanted to pursue a new relationship with Bastien. I just wanted to work on myself and take baby steps. But I did miss Bastien...a lot. **I hope you're well.** I shouldn't have sent the message at all, shouldn't interfere with his life when I was such a fucking mess, but my thumb hit send.

His dots were immediate, like he'd been on his phone when I texted. **Are you well, sweetheart?** His voice played in my head when I read the message, perfectly capturing his baritone and slight hint of playfulness.

I typed a message but then deleted it. Started over, trying to find a lighthearted answer instead of telling him the truth—that I'd hit rock bottom. **Yes.**

Don't lie to me.

My heart started to drum like it always did when he was near, like he was right at the back of my neck, his breaths across my skin. There was something about him that made me uneasy and the most comfortable I'd ever been at the same time. I didn't say anything, unsure how to respond to such assertiveness.

Where are you?

The bar.

His dots were long gone.

I suspected he was on his way here, that in a couple minutes, he would be the only customer at the bar. I put on a fake smile and did my best to look like everyone else, but I knew it would be impossible to do that when he was across from me. I'd quickly learned that it was easier to lie to strangers than to people you knew.

Less than ten minutes later, he walked inside, dressed in all black, his short sleeves showing all his muscles and the black ink over his thick arms, the cords down his forearms, the images of skulls and snakes and scorpions on his beautiful skin.

His eyes were on me the moment he walked in. He moved for where I stood at the bar, not taking a seat so he towered over me, his hands together when they rested on the surface that I'd just wiped down. And then he stared.

And stared and stared.

No one had ever stared at me like that, like I was all they could see.

It was hard to hold his look, to see the blue eyes that had flashed across my mind so many times in our separation, from my dreams to my waking moments. A warm sensation burned in my chest, and the longer it burned, the more it hurt. Something about this man—this stranger—elicited so much emotion in me.

He seemed to know that because he extended his palm forward, his knuckles against the counter.

I stared at the big hand that had touched me everywhere, that had carried me to his bed, that had held me when I fell asleep against his chest on the couch, that squeezed my ass in a way that made me feel possessed rather than objectified. I finally placed my hand in his and felt his fingers close around it and give it a nice squeeze.

It felt so nice... I couldn't even describe it.

"Sweetheart."

My eyes lifted to his, feeling that warmth in my chest again, falling deep into those blue eyes.

"It's gonna be okay."

We went to *Au Pied de Cochon* after I got off work, a restaurant I'd spent a lot of time in since my divorce, the perfect place for a smoke after a long day, for a late-night meal when I didn't have time to eat anything.

There were a few people in the restaurant, but it was mostly empty except for us and a couple other tables.

Bastien ordered a stiff drink, and I had a glass of wine and an appetizer.

It was nearly three in the morning, but Bastien didn't seem even slightly tired. He didn't have bags under his eyes, had a distinct clarity to his gaze that made it seem like he'd woken up just a few hours ago.

The drinks were brought to our table, along with the burrata I ordered.

Bastien didn't seem interested because he didn't touch it.

"I haven't eaten anything today."

"Then you should have ordered more than the burrata."

"I said I hadn't eaten, not that I was hungry." I grabbed a piece of bread and spooned the fresh cheese with the tomato on top, making my own version of bruschetta. I took a bite, struck by the subtle salt and the basil, the cheese so fresh it seemed to have been prepared just that hour.

With his fingers resting on the top of his short glass, his elbows on the table, he was a man far too big for such a small table. We were on the second level against the window, seeing the buildings lit up across the way.

I drank my glass of wine, enjoying the floral tones that masked the distinctiveness of the alcohol. After serving people fancy drinks all night, it was nice to enjoy one myself. I would have sat outside and enjoyed a cigarette if it weren't so cold, but the dampness in the air would probably give me a chill.

"We can talk about it or not talk about it," Bastien said. "Either is fine with me."

I looked down at my glass then his, seeing the tattoos on the backs of his fingers, Roman numerals. It started off at I on his pinkie and then made its way to V on his thumb. Both of his hands were that way. "What do the Roman numerals mean?" I lifted my gaze to his eyes.

He didn't look down at his hands to check what I meant. "The Fifth Republic."

My eyes searched his for more information.

"The second-longest reigning political system in France —our current political system."

I stared at his ink for another moment before I looked at him again. "And why is that important to you?"

He stared at me for a long time, his fingers resting on top of his glass. "Because that is the Republic that I serve."

I'd been submerged in a depression that was colder than the Arctic, but my head popped out of the water when I heard what he said, when I understood it was important, even though I didn't know why. "Adrien told me you're dangerous."

He didn't react like he'd been caught in the spotlight, like he was red-handed in the midst of a crime. Adrien's eyes had reacted in a distinctive way when I'd cornered him about Cecilia. He couldn't lie his way out of it. But Bastien didn't do that, didn't stiffen like a boy caught with his hand in the cookie jar. "I am dangerous," he said. "But not to you."

A warning flashed in my heart, but I ignored it—for better or worse. "How are you dangerous?"

He turned his attention elsewhere, surveying the other tables and deciding they were far enough away. "It's a long and complicated story, but this is the headline you're looking for—I kill people."

This was the part where I should walk out and not look back, but I sat there and stared, the burrata forgotten. Adrien made his living in his nefarious ways, but it was a victimless crime because no one got hurt. But Bastien looked me in the eye and told me the truth—bluntly. Perhaps I was focusing on the wrong thing here, but that kind of honesty was damn refreshing. "Thank you for telling me the truth."

The seriousness of his face softened, his mouth possessing a hint of a smile. "You'll get tired of my honesty after a while."

"I don't think I will." It meant a lot to me to have that kind of respect, to be privy to information that a normal man would have concealed. "Adrien says there was no one else, but I don't trust him. What I would give to hear his answer and know it's the truth..."

His smile faded and his eyes hardened, like I'd said the wrong thing.

"What?"

He gave a slight shake of his head. "Where do the two of you stand?"

Marriage was sacred, and I didn't blame anyone for wanting to fight for it until their dying breath. When I'd married Adrien, I assumed it would be forever. That we would have babies together, grow old together, and then be buried side by side in the cemetery. It was hard to accept defeat, but surrender felt like the right option for me. "It's over." It still made me sad to say that, to know that our relationship had been destroyed because he couldn't keep his dick in his pants until he came home to me. "I said I would try...but then we met with the marriage counselor, and it just went to shit."

"Why did it go to shit?"

My eyes dropped down, remembering how many times I'd thought about Bastien as I sat there, unable to get those blue eyes out of my goddamn mind. It had been as if he were there in the room, watching the whole thing unfold. "There was a vase on the corner of her desk, and she accidentally knocked it over."

He continued to stare at me, his fingers relaxed on the cool glass, giving no discernible reaction to that.

"Glass...everywhere."

He definitely had edges of arrogance, but he didn't display them now.

"Adrien helped her clean it up, but I still spotted pieces in corners...and I didn't say anything."

"And then you left?"

"Yeah. We talked at the apartment, and I pulled the plug. He accepted it this time—I think."

"And that was it? Nothing else was said?"

I studied his face, trying to understand why he continued to push the needle. "Should something else have been said?"

He brought the glass to his lips and took a drink. A long one, unnecessarily so. When he set it down, he licked his lips. An answer didn't seem forthcoming, like he'd somehow forgotten my question. "You made the right decision."

"I thought you were too biased to give advice?"

He smiled slightly then looked at the glass sitting at the bottom of his fingertips. "In this case, my advice is pretty fucking objective."

Bastien walked me to the lobby door hidden between the two rows of hedges. There was a mist in the air, visible in the lights outside the buildings, drops of rain so light they floated like snow. "I'll leave you here."

I scanned my phone into the computer so the lock on the door released. It was as heavy as the gates to an old keep, something that couldn't be broken down by a herd of Clydesdales. I looked at him standing in the mist like the cold didn't bother him at all, didn't leave bumps on his arms as his body tightened to stop the heat from escaping. "Why?"

That boyish smile moved in that rugged, manly face. "I assumed you needed some time."

"I do." There wasn't a word to accurately describe the way I felt, a mixture of sorrow and unstoppable rage. There was a special kind of anger felt by women who had to leave their lying husbands. Wished I knew what that word was. "But I also want you to stay." How could I be so heartbroken over one man but so desperate for another? How could I want this man so much that it made me sick when we were apart?

"I'm trying to be a gentleman, but I've never been good at it."

"I don't want a gentleman," I said as I continued to hold on to the door. "I want you."

His smile widened like I'd vanquished his restraint. He moved to the door, and even though it weighed a hundred pounds at least, he opened it like it weighed nothing. We entered the warmth of the lobby and began the walk up the circular staircase, the carpet an olive green with white flowers in the center.

We made it to the top floor, and I scanned the door to get it unlocked. My apartment was quiet and cold because I turned off the heat before I left. The first thing I did was move to the thermostat and turn it up so I wouldn't freeze during the night.

I was about to drop my jacket over the back of the chair but changed my mind. "I'm so fucking cold."

"Here." He pulled his shirt over his head, revealing a body so hard it looked like a sculpture rather than living flesh. "It's a lot warmer than that jacket."

I hesitated before I dropped the coat, immediately feeling the frigid air attack me like a swarm of needles. When I removed my top and unclasped my bra, my tits were hard and my nipples looked sharper than any of the knives in my kitchen.

He stared straight at my tits. Didn't try to be discreet because discreet wasn't his style.

I pulled on his black tee, and just as he'd said, it was as warm as a furnace. My skin immediately bubbled into bumps because it felt like a steaming bath. I stepped out of my boots and left my socks on. My jeans came next. I'd never undressed next to my dining table before.

He moved into me, his big hands sliding underneath my shirt and squeezing my hips, so hot they felt like heated oven mitts.

"You're so warm." My arms circled his back, and my cheek rested against his chest. I felt like I was sunbathing on a summer day, soaking in the heat on the pool deck. I'd been frigid just a second ago, but now it felt like I'd stepped into the desert.

His hands scooped over my ass, and he lifted me into him before he carried me into the bedroom. I'd rented the loft at the top because it was cheaper, and it was cheaper because most of the walls slanted in and made it hard to stand upright in most places. It was no place for someone like him, a man taller than the average man, who took up most of the hallway with his bulkiness. That was especially true in the bedroom, but he navigated it effortlessly and rolled me onto the bed, his body acting as a fur blanket and smothering the heat against me.

He pulled the blankets over us before he slid below, yanking my panties off before he pressed his kiss against the warmest part of my body.

I sucked in a breath as I arched my back, the duvet cover at my shoulders to keep me warm, the bison-sized man underneath the sheets so stifling hot, he acted as a heater to warm the entire bed and me with it.

His arms hooked underneath my thighs, and he kissed my lips as hard as he kissed my mouth, with a possessiveness that made me feel like I was his even though I was technically married to someone else.

I moaned in the dark, one hand moving to the headboard behind me, my fingers on the other grasping his short hair beneath the covers. I quickly forgot about the cold when he did incredible things with his mouth, when he kissed me like it was an honor rather than an obligation. I felt it fast, felt the heat roll over the hills and head straight for me. "Wait, stop."

Instead of ignoring me and doing what he wanted, he moved up my body, kissing my belly that was exposed from his lifted shirt. He tugged the sheets off so he could move over me, his bare back to the ceiling.

My hands moved for his jeans, and I unbuttoned them fast.

He smirked once he understood why I'd asked him to stop. He kicked his bottoms away and left the clothing somewhere at the bottom of the bed and then he rose over me, his knees separating my thighs, our bodies coming together like they'd known each other for years rather than weeks.

I moaned as I squeezed his torso with my knees, as my arms hooked over his shoulders and brought him in close. His touch always made me burn from the inside out, made me burst like a lit firework. I dug my hand into his hair as I felt him kiss my collarbone then give my shoulder a gentle bite with his teeth.

His hand slid into the back of my hair then he forced my face toward his, his lips kissing one corner of my mouth then the other, his rock-hard dick inside me and pulsing. Then he started to rock into me. His thumb brushed my cheeks, his blue eyes hard and almost angry with their intensity.

"Oh Jesus..." I grabbed on to the bicep of one of his arms, my fingers digging into his hardness like a crevasse on a cliff. I planted my other hand on his chest, and I felt my body jerk over and over as he gave me hard thrusts like a piston in an engine, erasing any trace that Adrien or any other had been there, erasing the hurt caused by lesser men. I was already there the second his mouth sealed over my sex, so I burned like the fire and I came around his big dick with whimpers and tears.

"Fuck." He tugged my hair, bringing my eyes to his. "You're beautiful when you come."

My hand slid up the tattoos on his neck, and I palmed his face. "So are you." I dug my nails into his ass, wanting his seed inside me, to sit there and keep me warm through the night, to mark me as his when I no longer belonged to anyone.

He gripped the back of my head to keep me in place, and he pounded into me like a bulldozer into a building, demolishing it into pieces, leaving nothing but a wreck behind. His face tinted red, a blotchiness moved across his collarbone and chest, and the veins in his neck were so taut they looked like tightropes. A deep moan escaped his throat when he released, giving me a look so hard it was like he hated me, his jawline sharper than ever.

I winced as I took it, taking that big dick and its explosion at the end of my channel, but it didn't compare to the satisfaction of receiving him, of feeling that connection that I'd only felt with him. With Adrien, I'd enjoyed the sex, but his climax was never a specific turn-on. But with Bastien, everything about it turned me on. Maybe because I knew how much it would piss off Adrien if he knew, not just that I was sleeping with someone else, but that I was begging him to come inside me like a starving beggar pleaded for food.

It was the first time we finished in a single round. He rolled off me onto the other pillow, his muscular body visible because the sheets were at our waists. The bedroom was filled with warmth because of him, not because I'd cranked up the heater a couple minutes ago.

I still wore his t-shirt and didn't want to take it off. It felt like silk against my skin even though it was ordinary cotton. But he wouldn't be able to leave unless I took it off, unless he walked down the street with his bare chest, and if that happened, then the city of Paris owed me a big fucking thank-you card.

I propped myself up and started to pull it off.

He grabbed the bottom and tugged it down. "You're fine. It looks better on you anyway."

"No, it doesn't," I said with a laugh because he filled out his clothes so damn well...and his naked skin too. "I assumed you had somewhere to be."

"No." His arm circled my lower back, and he brought me in close, hiking my leg over his hip, his hard stare locked on mine from just inches away. "You think I'm gonna let you freeze to death?" That boyish smile returned, a hint of playfulness that lightened his intensity.

Like a balloon inflated inside me, my lips started to rise for the sky. "You are warm..." My hand moved across his chest, tracing a tattoo just beneath his collarbone. Adrien didn't have a single tattoo. None of the guys I'd been with had any ink. I usually went for clean-cut men who wore slacks to work.

Bastien was nothing like any of them.

"I'll keep you warm," he said. "But it's gonna cost you."

"Yeah?"

He gripped my ass cheek and squeezed before he gave it a gentle spank. "Oh yeah."

"Sounds like a fair trade to me."

His fingers gently grazed my thigh, exploring the soft skin to the back of my knee before he came back to my ass again. His blue eyes stared at me, locked on my gaze with more confidence than I'd ever felt, even on my best day. His aura was so still and so calm, like an undisturbed lake that didn't have a single ripple, the surface dark so the contents beneath remained a mystery. "You're a damn beautiful woman."

I felt the softness flood into my heart and pull at my eyes. Felt myself feel something at a line he probably said to all women—but of course, I believed he only said it to me.

"And don't you fucking forget it."

Chapter 10

Bastien

I sat in the back of the SUV across the street, smoking my cigar with the window cracked, waiting for the show to start.

A black Hummer came around the corner, going over sixty kilometers per hour, and crashed straight into the iron gate, making one door break off the hinges while the other swung inward and knocked over the guards positioned outside. Some of them looked injured, others dead, and the others who weren't either were smart enough to take off.

"That's my cue, boys." I hopped out of the car, crossed the street, strode past where the gates had been, and walked right up to the front door. It was also made of iron, the doors thirteen feet tall and pretentiously grand. Before I motioned to my guys to break it down, one of the staff was dumb enough to open the door.

"Thanks." I shoved him aside as I made my way inside. "Adrien!" I stormed into his house like it was my own, walked through the entryway that Fleur must have walked in hundreds of times during the years she lived here. "Get your pussy-ass down here, bitch."

In a rush, he appeared at the top of the stairs on the next floor. "Jesus fucking Christ, are you insane?"

"Abso-fucking-lutely." The cigar was still in the corner of my mouth, the smoke drifting to where he stood at the top of the stairs. "Now get your ass down here, or I'll blow these goddamn stairs and watch you break your neck." I pulled the grenade from my pocket, the pin still intact—for now.

He looked like a deer in the headlights, about to lose his lunch from the sheer panic. But he made the right decision and came down the stairs with haste before he faced me. "What the fuck—"

I punched him in the face, and he fell back and hit his head on the bottom step.

"Get up."

He winced as he raised his head and checked the wound with his palm, getting blood on the skin. "You could have killed me."

"I know." I kicked him. "Get up."

He growled before he got to his feet and faced me, blood dripping down his neck and into his shirt.

"You didn't tell her."

He actually had the audacity to look angry when he realized she'd come back to me the second he was gone. "She's still my wife, asshole."

There were so many fucking things I wanted to say. So many ways I could prove that she was mine and she *wanted* to be mine—in no uncertain terms. But I respected the hell out of that woman. Would rather let him win the argument than betray her privacy and dignity. "I warned you what would happen if you didn't tell her."

"I was going to when she agreed to work on the relationship, but now that she's out, it doesn't matter."

"It does fucking matter," I snapped. "Be a man and tell her—or I will."

"Why would I hurt her?"

"So she knows she made the right choice—and she never has to look back and wonder. So she knows that her marriage failed because her husband was a piece of shit cockroach, not because she wasn't enough. So she knows she deserves a hell of a lot better than a punk-ass bitch like you. That's why you're going to tell her."

He continued to bleed, continued to stand there and look angry—like I was in the wrong.

"You think I won't kill you?"

His eyes narrowed.

"Because I will."

"I didn't betray the code."

"The law is always up for interpretation—and I'm the sole interpreter. Causing undue harm can have a lot of different meanings. And I'd say you've caused Fleur a lot of unnecessary harm. These are your two options. You can tell her what you did, not on the phone, but straight to her goddamn face—or I'll tell her and hand you over to the boys in the catacombs so they can make you their next satanic sacrifice."

"You're fucking crazy—"

"You have no idea, asshole." I pulled the cigar out of my mouth and tossed it on his rug, where it continued to burn. A smirk stretched across my face. "You have a week to grow a new set of balls."

I knew she was at work, so I stopped by Silencio after getting shit done. Her tits were perky as hell in her little top, and she had long hair in a high ponytail that gave her an oomph of attitude that was hot as fuck.

A guy seated at the bar had eyes for her too, because when she turned around to grab a bottle from a high shelf, he stared straight at her ass.

I would have done the same if I were him, but she was my woman as far as I was concerned.

She came back to where he sat and poured him his drink. "Can I get you anything else?"

"A phone number would be nice."

She chuckled—actually chuckled like it was fucking ridiculous—and her brush-off was so ice-cold I didn't even need to do anything.

His face went pale. I could see it in the mirror. He shut up and drank from his glass, his face red from his bruised ego.

I took a seat a few chairs down.

After she handed him his tab, she spotted me, and a smile brighter than the lights of Paris hit me like the spotlight from the Eiffel Tower. She sauntered over with her hour-glass frame, her eyes catlike because she'd done her makeup differently. She made my drink, a scotch on the rocks, a double. "This one's on the house—just because you're fucking hot." She winked at me, so sexy when she was confident in who she was, and then moved down to the next customer. It was a busy night, so she didn't have as much time to chat as she normally did.

I felt a stare on the side of my face, so I turned to look.

The guy she'd turned down just looked at me.

"She's my girl," I explained, granting him a bit of mercy.

Thoroughly embarrassed by his failed shot, he just left, leaving his full drink there along with his paid tab.

Fleur continued to help everyone else who wanted a drink, managing to work the room without appearing stressed about it.

I didn't need her attention. I was perfectly content drinking my scotch and watching her work, her tits unbelievable in that top and her ass ready for a bite in that skirt. Sometimes she would pass and give me the eye.

A woman took a seat at the bar beside me, an attractive blonde in a little cocktail dress. "Whatcha drinking?"

It took me a second to realize she was talking to me. "Scotch."

"I like a man who enjoys a stiff drink."

I ignored her and turned back to Fleur, her back to me as she grabbed new bottles from the cabinet.

"I'm Denise—"

"I've got a woman." My eyes followed Fleur as I brought the glass to my lips and took a drink, the scotch already halfway gone.

The blonde continued to sit there like she'd never been rejected in her life and didn't know what to do.

Fleur walked over to help her. "What can I get you, girl?"

She hesitated before she answered. "Vodka cranberry."

Fleur pulled out a glass and threw the drink together before she slid the full glass to her. "Anything else?"

The blonde shook her head.

Fleur brought the transaction machine to her, showed her the bill on the screen, and processed her payment. The blonde returned to the table where she sat with her friends. Fleur gave no indication she knew what had transpired between the blonde and me and continued with her shift.

I finished my glass then tapped it against the counter. "Sweetheart."

Her eyes lit up when she looked at me, and she made me another drink, holding my gaze while her hands moved, a fucking pro. Then she walked off and continued to help everyone else who squeezed into the bar, either wanting a drink or just to get close to her.

It took an hour for the bar to quiet down.

"I'm gonna have to cut you off, sir." She came to where I sat at the bar and leaned forward, her elbows on the edge of the bar, her tits practically falling out of her top.

I looked down and stared—purposely and intently. "Because of my disorderly conduct of staring at your tits and ass all night?" My eyes lifted to hers again, my glass empty in front of me, the ice cubes still fully formed at the bottom of the glass.

"Because I'm going home with you—and we close in ten minutes."

The smile she pulled from me was out of my control. She was a magician, saying the magic words to make me do her bidding. "Get me the bill, sweetheart."

She moved to the register and printed out the bill before she set it in front of me.

I slipped a wad of bills inside and watched her close up for the night. I was pleased she wanted to come to my place because I didn't care for her apartment. The loft was not suitable for someone like me, who had to duck to navigate the sloping walls in every room. And not to be a dick, but I was used to the finer things in life, and her apartment was simply below my standards.

She finished her cleanup and closed the registers before she walked out. There were other workers there finishing up in the kitchen, so they would lock the doors after they turned off the lights.

We stepped into the cold night, and I texted my driver to get us. I slid my arm around the small of her back, and I pulled her into me as we stood on the curb, keeping her warm against me. She'd put on her coat, but the bumps on her chest told me she was cold.

She melted into me like a piece of chocolate, her cheek against my chest, her arms around my waist like a little girl with her teddy bear.

I looked down the street and saw the SUV turn the corner and approach us where we stood on the sidewalk. The driver didn't open the door for me since I'd specifically told him not to because I could open my own fucking door. I got her in the back seat, and then we headed to my place in the 7th arrondissement.

She looked out the back window, her coat tight around her to keep warm.

I reached for the heater in the center and cranked it up for her.

When she saw what I did, a little smile moved over her face and she gave me this look...like she appreciated the small things.

I wondered if Adrien was ever as thoughtful. Probably not.

Fifteen minutes later, we entered the gates of my property and walked into the house.

"Hungry?" I asked.

"I don't know." She walked beside me as we headed to the stairs. "It's late."

I texted my butler and asked him to prepare dinner. "It's not late—at least not for me." We entered my bedroom, the lights low on the dimmer, a fire roaring in the fireplace because I'd told my butler to prepare it before I arrived.

She looked around the room, taking it in like she'd never seen it before, but she didn't issue a comment. She seemed to be warm before she took off her coat and purse and set them over one of the armchairs in the sitting room. "You have a beautiful home. I don't think I said that before."

"Thank you." She hadn't asked me about my wealth or mentioned it at all. She was either too classy or she really didn't care. "The building used to have several different apartments, but I renovated it into a single home."

She gave a slight nod. "That's an ambitious endeavor."

"I'm an ambitious man." My butler had left a silver platter on the table, a bottle of wine and two glasses. I uncorked it and filled both glasses before I took a seat in front of the fire. Then I looked at her and patted the spot beside me.

She smiled before she walked over to me in that little skirt with her tight shirt tucked in, showing all the right curves in all the right places, a woman with hips and tits and an ass I could grab on to. She took the spot beside me and crossed her legs, her hand moving to my thigh in my jeans, her face close to my chest.

I moved my arm over her shoulders and scooped her into me, keeping her close, her hair brushing my lips.

She snuggled into me and looked at the fire. "This is nice."

I'd be all over her right now, but dinner was on the way and I didn't want her naked on my couch when Gerard came to the door. So I held her, glancing down her top even though I already knew how her tits looked because I'd sucked on her nipples until they were raw. "How was work?"

"Shit," she said. "Until you walked in. I need to find something else."

"What kind of experience do you have?"

"Not much. I was at university when I met Adrien, but I never finished," she said. "Stupid on my part."

"Why is that stupid?"

"Because I believed him when he said he would take care of me—like a fucking idiot."

"That's not stupid."

She released a sheathed chuckle. "Never trust a man to take care of you."

"That's not the lesson," I said. "Never trust the *wrong* man to take care of you. And you are entitled to the community assets of your marriage in the divorce."

"Sure, but I don't want that."

"Why?" Most women would want to bleed their husbands dry as punishment for their infidelity. Would want to hurt him where it hurt most—his bank account.

"Because I loved him for him, not his money, and one day when he realizes women only want him because of the fancy dinners and the nice cars and the big house...he'll realize he threw away a woman who actually gave a damn about him."

I wanted her to take some kind of compensation, even a small sum to have a decent apartment, but I admired her principles.

"So, he can keep the money—and shove it up his ass."

A quiet knock sounded on the door. My butler didn't wait for me to answer it before he opened the door and wheeled in the cart, just like room service at a hotel. He didn't look at us on the couch before he approached the dining table near the terrace and set up our dinner, putting down the white tablecloth and placing the dishes there along with the butter and the basket of bread. Then he wheeled the cart out again and disappeared.

We sat together at the dining table and ate our dinner, a soup and salad for her and a rare steak with potatoes for me.

She seemed to like it because she was focused on her food the entire time, like she'd been hungry all night but didn't have time to eat. Last time I saw her at *Au Pied de Cochon,* she barely touched her burrata. She was either that hungry or in better spirits altogether.

I stared at her across from me, seeing the way she dragged the bottom of her spoon over the edge of her bowl, trying to cut off the cheese from her French onion soup. She dipped a piece of bread into it before she took a bite. That was when she noticed my stare, and she stilled when she realized she had my attention. "What?"

"I like watching you eat."

"Why?" She dipped the bread into the soup again and soaked it before she finished the second half of the bread slice.

I chose not to give an answer, because I really didn't have

one. "You said you lost your friends and family in the separation. What of your parents?"

"They're gone." She continued to eat like the loss didn't bother her.

As it didn't seem to cause her pain, I didn't say I was sorry for her loss. I wanted to know more, but since she didn't elaborate on her own, I didn't want to pry. But I could tell there was more to the situation by how closed off she was. "No siblings?"

"No." Abrupt and cold, there was definitely more there. "What about you?"

"I never knew my father. My mother is still around."

Her coldness evaporated when the attention had been shifted to me. "Does she live in Paris?"

"Yes—Champs-Elysees."

"That's a nice area."

"It is." I'd bought her a house so she could have something that no one could take from her. She had a butler in case she needed anything, like groceries or someone to pick up her medications.

"Are you close with her?"

"I talk to her once every couple of weeks." It was a lot of the same conversations over and over, superficial bullshit like the weather and politics and her nosy neighbors next door. Nothing substantial. Nothing real.

Fleur seemed to have the same kind of awareness I did, to know when the conversation had gone as far as I was willing for it to go. "Do you have any siblings?"

It was a simple question but a hard one. A question that made me pause for several seconds as I tried to decide how I wanted to answer it.

Her salad plate was clean and her soup bowl was empty, but she continued to soak up the remains with the bread. "Was that blonde hitting on you?" When her piece of bread had soaked up as much soup as it could, she placed it in her mouth to chew. She either changed the subject when she understood my unease, or she simply grew impatient—but I suspected it was the former.

"Yes." Most people chose to mold the truth into the version they wanted it to be, but I'd never tampered with it. Being brutally honest and accepting the consequences of that was far easier to me.

She held my stare for a second before she dipped her bread into the bowl again, doing her best to get whatever drops remained. She asked no follow-up questions to my answer. It was unclear if she was jealous about that—or if she cared at all.

This woman was something else.

"You said you kill people. Can I ask you more about that?"

"Go ahead, sweetheart."

When she realized the soup was all gone, she gave me her full attention. "Does that mean you're a hit man? Someone people hire to kill the people they hate?"

"No."

Her eyes narrowed in confusion, but she didn't ask me to elaborate.

"Have you ever heard of the Fifth Republic Conspiracy?"

She considered the question before she shook her head. "No."

"Well, it's not a conspiracy—it's the truth," I said. "There are two levels of the Senate, the Senate and the National Assembly. But there's actually a third level—the French Emperors. I'm the first of five. It's a secret society, essentially."

She was still as she listened, giving no reaction to what I said like she needed more time to process that information. She might not follow politics at all, might just know President Martin was the current president and nothing else.

"In the last few decades, crime has become rampant in France, particularly Paris. Trafficking, organized crime, drug operations and possession, sacrificial cults out in the wilds—all that shit has become a problem. It used to be a safe place for travelers, but now it's become a higher-risk area, particularly for the vulnerable, especially women. Rather than vanquish all those organizations, I police them."

She hadn't blinked since I'd started talking, completely enraptured by this information.

"They continue their operations—but under the rules of the Fifth Republic. In exchange for their cooperation, they're allowed to continue their criminal activities without fear of apprehension. And the Fifth Republic is compensated through taxes and tariffs."

She didn't ask any questions, either because she was in shock or she didn't want further information.

I drank my wine as I watched her process all this information with a preternatural calmness.

"How are you compensated?"

"I claim a percentage of the taxes and tariffs."

"How do you do this all by yourself?"

"I don't." I had men on my payroll everywhere, had snitches in the midst of the organizations I policed, had my own headquarters and my own men to do my bidding, and also had the police force if I needed it. "There's a president of the Senate, there's a president of France, and there's a president of the French Emperors—which is me."

If her husband weren't a criminal, she probably wouldn't have believed any of that and would have bolted out of there as fast as possible. And maybe she remembered the night we met, when I'd handled those idiots as they'd tried to rob the bar with machetes. That was just a slow night for me.

"*Homines ex codice.*" She said the same words to me that I'd said to others. "I remember you said that at the bar to those guys...like they were supposed to know what that meant."

"Man of the code," I said. "Roughly translated from Latin."

"And what is the code?"

"Not to harm innocents. And not to endanger women. They can conduct their clandestine affairs all they want, as long as they do those things and pay their taxes. Seems like a simple ask, but there was pushback. About fifteen years ago, there was a drug operation outside of France that used trafficked women as free labor. It caught on, and more men started to do it. We had so many missing persons reports that the United Nations classified us as an unsafe country for travelers. Tourism suffered, and the economy hit an all-time low—other than during the Second World War. The third level of the Senate was formed, and I was elected to the position, and the other Four Emperors aid me in this duty. I consider myself a patriot of this country, a distant relative of Napoleon Bonaparte, so I felt compelled to do it."

She was quiet for a very long time. Probably minutes. "And why did they choose you?"

"I was well-connected in the criminal underworld in my previous profession."

"Which was?"

I smiled slightly. "A hit man."

She continued to stare at me with that steel-like gaze, her thoughts a mystery.

I was afraid that she would leave and never come back. That she would realize I was dangerous by association and she should avoid me at all costs. But I wouldn't lie to her—not even to keep her.

"You need not fear me, sweetheart."

Her eyes had wandered elsewhere in her thoughts. It took her a moment to look at me again. "I don't."

"Good."

"I probably should, but I don't."

I watched her green eyes, saw the way she argued with herself on the inside, the way she tried to understand the severity of her predicament.

"I just don't really care...about anything."

———

She straddled my hips, her skirt still on and bunched around her hips, her thong on the rug in front of the fire. She pulled her shirt off over her head, her hair catching the fabric and being pulled until it came free.

Before the shirt was gone, I had already unclasped her bra and set her tits free. Her perky, perfect tits. I moaned when I saw them then sealed my mouth over one nipple and sucked hard enough to make her wince.

I squeezed her ass under her skirt then gave her a hard smack before I squeezed it again. "Fuck, sweetheart." I kissed her collarbone then her neck, digging my hand into her hair and yanking her head back to expose more of her throat. "You turn me the fuck on." I spanked her ass again before I lifted her to get my dick inside, so eager to feel that snug channel that would come all over me. I guided her on top of me then gripped her hip as I pulled her onto me, moaning when I felt that tight little pussy seal me like an airlock.

She took a deep breath when she felt me fill her, and then she moaned, moaned like it was the best dick she'd ever had, rolled her head back and closed her eyes like the sexiest little thing ever.

She planted her hands against my chest, and she arched her back farther than I thought was possible. Her stomach was tight because she flexed, her perfect tits in my face, and she started to ride me nice and slow, taking her time, looking into my eyes with her lips slightly parted, taking my dick like it was a fucking honor.

"You like that dick, sweetheart?"

Her answer was breathless. "Yes."

I gripped her hips, my thumbs over her belly, and I pushed my hips up to meet her when she came down, the two of us fucking better than we breathed. My hands stretched over her ass where it poked out from her skirt, and I squeezed hard, loving the feel of that meat in my grip.

She started to bounce faster, rolling her hips when she reached my base and coming back up again, her tits shifting with her movements. The fire was in the hearth behind her, her beautiful skin aglow from the flames, and soon, I saw a sheen of sweat over her fair skin. "I fucking love this dick."

I spanked her ass hard. "Attagirl."

We were moving hard and fast together, and like any man, I was at the mercy of my dick, this fine piece of woman bringing me to my knees. She hadn't reached her peak, while I was right at the finish line, so I did what I had to do.

I slipped my hand under her skirt and rubbed that clit like my life depended on it.

She moaned louder than before, her nails slicing my chest, her nipples hardening at the touch.

I licked my thumb before I rubbed her hard, making her hips convulse like she'd lost her motor functions. She panted and moaned, and then she grabbed on to my shoulder and lifted herself onto the balls of her feet, holding the weight of her body on her thighs, and bounced on my dick harder. "Jesus fucking Christ." It was like she did it on purpose, tried to beat me at some sick game. She raised herself to the top of my dick then dropped down all the way to the base before she did it again, her cream building up and dripping over my balls, her slickness a mess on the couch.

So fucking hot.

But I won the game—and she came all over me. She fell into my chest and locked her arms around my neck as she convulsed, moaning in my ear, her tears catching on the skin of my neck.

I spanked her again and again, making her cry out as she finished, making that beautiful ass red and welted from my handprint. Because she'd done all the work up to this point, I rolled her over and pinned her in the corner of the couch, bending her so I could pound into her, my ass on display to the fire, my dick balls deep in that slick paradise. I pounded into her so hard I made the couch shift over on the rug.

Her cries were muffled because of how she was folded, her hands grabbing on to my arm and shoulder, whatever she could latch on to as she took the pounding of a lifetime. Then she took the bomb out of the cannon, the mound of come I'd been wanting to give her since the last load.

"You love my come, don't you, sweetheart?"

"Yes." She hooked her legs around me and squeezed, locking her ankles together at the top of my waist so I couldn't leave. "I want more."

My dick was still hard even though I'd found my release. That didn't happen a lot, but with her, it seemed to happen almost every time, like my dick didn't get the memo that the fire was over. "Then beg for it." I started to grind into her, but moved slowly, feeling our slickness slide past each other.

"Please..." She cupped the back of my neck and brought me close, kissing me hard on the mouth. "Bastien, please make me come again." She didn't shy away from my commands—like she wanted to beg. Like she loved all this dirty talk. Like she wanted me to spank her until she couldn't sit.

I started to rock into her again, moving fast, burrowing her into the corner of the couch.

She stroked my jawline before she caressed my bottom lip with her thumb, touching me like she wanted every part of me but couldn't have it all at the same time. "Yes... like that."

Chapter 11

Fleur

When I woke up, I was in his bed, but I couldn't remember how I got there. The last memory I had was of us together on the couch, lying there as the fire burned low. He'd pulled a blanket over me that had been over the back of the couch to keep me warm.

He must have carried me to bed at some point.

The mattress was soft, the sheets were like silk, and it was warm. I reached for him beside me, but realized I was alone. The curtains were closed over the window, and when I glanced at the clock on his nightstand, I saw it was noon.

I lay there for a while because his bed was just so damn comfortable. I hoped I hadn't overstayed my welcome by sleeping over. Maybe I should have just taken a taxi home. Didn't want to put pressure on something that was supposed to be casual.

My phone was on the nightstand, so he must have put it there. When I checked my messages, I saw that some of my friends wanted to get together, no doubt to tell me that leaving Adrien was a big mistake. Even if he did cheat, his mistress was on the street and I was in the palace, so what did it matter?

It mattered to me.

I finally got up and peed in his bathroom, and when I stepped back into the bedroom, I saw that the curtains were open because he'd joined me. His back was to me from where he stood by the window, wearing workout shorts and sneakers, his entire back ripped and flexed from his workout. He turned to look at me, stopping to give me a once-over because I was still naked.

I stared at him just as hard because his skin was red and his muscles were plump, probably from lifting trucks and buildings. He had a shake in his hand, probably a recovery drink full of a shit-ton of protein. "Morning."

"Morning." He took another drink before he capped it and set it on the dresser. He walked over to me and bent his neck down to kiss me as he squeezed my lower back. "Breakfast will be here in a couple minutes. I'm gonna shower."

"Breakfast?"

"Yeah. Hungry?"

"I mean...I'm always hungry for pancakes."

He smirked before he walked into the bathroom. He showered, and I fixed myself up, washing away the smeared makeup that made me look like I had two black eyes. I didn't want to wear my skirt and my skintight top during breakfast, so I took one of his shirts and put on the pair of socks he'd taken off the night before. They stretched all the way to my knees, black like the shirt that fit me like a loose blanket.

Gerard had set the table in the other room. It was overcast and a little windy, so we didn't sit on the terrace. I took a seat before Bastien, who was putting on some clothes in his bedroom. I'd just poured myself a cup of coffee when my phone lit up with a text message from Adrien.

I need to speak with you.

Just seeing his name on the screen pissed me off. I was having a beautiful morning with a gorgeous man who gave out orgasms like candy on Halloween—and the last thing I wanted to do was think about the man who wasted my goddamn time. *Fuck off.*

Fleur, come on.

Go fuck yourself.

Would you rather me show up to your apartment?

We can speak in court when I divorce your ass.

"Everything okay?"

I nearly jumped at the sound of his voice. He'd taken the seat across from me without my noticing. He was bare-chested and in just his sweatpants, a fucking man treat, but I couldn't enjoy it in my annoyance. "Yeah, everything's fine." I swiped down and turned on the Do Not Disturb feature because I did not want Adrien to disrupt this morning any further.

Bastien continued to stare at me like he didn't believe any of that, especially since he'd watched me silence my phone, something he'd never seen me do before. But he grabbed the pot and filled his mug with hot coffee.

I felt compelled to answer the question truthfully, and I wasn't sure why. "Adrien wants to speak to me. About what, I don't fucking know, nor do I care. I'm filing those divorce papers, and if he gets the judge to deny it, I swear to god—"

"He won't deny it—not this time." He drank from his mug, enjoying his coffee black while I flooded mine with cream, and then removed the silver dome over his breakfast, poached eggs with grilled mushrooms and spinach and bacon.

167

"Thanks."

"He shouldn't have blocked it in the first place. If a woman wants to leave, let her go."

"So, if you were in this situation, you wouldn't fight for her?"

He ate with his arms on the table, taking big bites with that big mouth. "If I fucked around on her, I wouldn't deserve her anyway. The decent thing to do is let her go so she can find someone who can give her what I can't. But this hypothetical question is stupid because I wouldn't fuck around in the first place. Women are not as complicated as we make them out to be."

"Have you been in a relationship before?" I really didn't know much about him. The more time we spent together and the better I got to know him, the more I realized I didn't know much at all.

"Not really."

"Not really?"

"I've had a couple long-term flings, but that hardly qualifies as a relationship."

"What constitutes long-term?"

"A week or so." He continued to eat, scarfing down his food and dragging a piece of bread across his plate to get the last of the yolk that was left behind.

I'd been fucking him for a couple weeks. I wasn't sure how much longer it would last, but I knew the fire would burn out at some point. He was a nice distraction—a really nice distraction. He made me feel good about myself, quieted the voice in my head, chased away the depression that made my bones brittle.

"What about you?"

I lifted the lid over my food and saw the treasure beneath, fluffy blueberry pancakes with bacon and poached eggs with a side of toast. When I cut my fork into the eggs, the yolk immediately began to run. "I was in my ho phase before I settled down with Adrien. Really enjoying my twenties..."

He smirked slightly as he ate, having no judgment at all. "I like that."

"You like that I was a ho?"

"I like that you did what the fuck you wanted without giving a damn."

I'd never heard a guy say that. Adrien was always uncomfortable with my body count.

"It's why you fuck so good."

"I fuck so good because you're really hot."

His smile widened, dimples forming in his cheeks,

looking so handsome in the morning light. He relaxed in the chair and drank from his mug.

I drenched my pancakes in syrup and ate the fluffy goodness. In my apartment, I scavenged for whatever I could find in the cabinets and the fridge. I had no one there to whip me up a feast.

"I want to ask you something." He turned serious, the smile from my compliment fading.

"Okay," I said between bites.

"Am I revenge sex?"

"Revenge sex?" I asked.

"Are you fucking me to get back at Adrien?" he asked. "Your answer won't bother me, I'm just curious."

I hadn't really thought of my actions too deeply. I was just moving through life, going from hit to hit, whatever kept out the sorrow. "No. When I saw you walk into the bar..." I didn't even know how to describe it. "I thought you were the sexiest man I'd ever seen. Until that moment, I couldn't even imagine being with anyone else, regardless of what Adrien did to me. But then I saw you...and I was lost."

He had no reaction to that, just listening to me, his fingers around the handle of his mug as his arm rested on the table.

"But I won't deny that I'm running from my misery, and fucking you is the best way to do that. You're the best antidepressant I've ever taken."

He watched me eat my food, crystal-blue eyes locked on my face as if transfixed. The stare lasted for seconds before he brought the mug to his lips and took a drink. Then a hint of a smile appeared there, subtle and handsome. "I'm glad to be of service, sweetheart."

A few days passed before Adrien texted me again. *Fleur, I really need to talk to you.*

I ignored him.

I'm coming by.

What part of fuck off do you not understand?

Fleur, I wouldn't bother you unless it was important.

Important to you...

Can I please come by?

You'd better be dying.

His dots came and went, starting and then disappearing before his answer hit the screen. *I suspect I'll be dead when the conversation is over.*

That both intrigued me—and scared me.

My shift starts at 7, so you better get here before then.

I'll be there soon.

I sat at the round dining table and tossed my phone onto the surface. My heart beat faster than it had a moment ago, full of adrenaline and dread. There was no escape from reality. The only time I felt a reprieve was when I was in the arms of a drop-dead gorgeous man with a magical dick. When I wasn't with him, the world was in shades of gray. Everything felt mundane and mediocre... and sad. Whenever I was alone with my thoughts, I was suffocated by my loneliness. Adrien had two brothers and sisters-in-law and nieces and nephews and parents who thought the world of him—even when he'd cheated on me. My friends were his friends, and they wanted me to take him back. That way, they wouldn't have to choose sides in the divorce. They didn't actually give a damn about my pain.

I became so lost in my thoughts that I forgot about the sounds of the bustling city through the cracked window, the ambulance sirens when they passed down the road. I barely noticed the sound of the door when it opened down the hallway.

When I looked up, Adrien was there, dressed in his typical business attire as if he'd had a meeting right before this. He gave me a glance over with sad eyes, like a dog that knew he had done something wrong. He hesitated before he took a seat in the chair, one ankle resting on the opposite knee, his hands in his lap, looking anywhere but at me.

When a moment turned into two and then several, I broke the silence. "You came here to say something?" I found it ironic that I'd done nothing wrong, yet I was the one who'd lost everything. I lived in a shitty apartment alone while he kept the palace, his reputation, and everyone that mattered.

He released a quiet sigh as he continued to avoid my gaze. It took him a moment to look at me, his eyes over-full with pain. "You asked me if there had been anyone else..." His eyes faltered again, the fear making him lose his spine. "I lied."

The adrenaline that spiked was hot, white-hot. When I thought I couldn't be any angrier, I was proven wrong. My visceral instinct was to rip him apart with my words, but when I took a breath before I released the fire, I decided to let it go instead. Because it really didn't matter. "How many were there?"

He was too much of a coward to look at me. "A couple instances..."

"Couple means two. You know that, right? So, was it two or more than two?"

He clenched his jaw like he wanted to grind his teeth into sand.

"You're the one who decided to come clean, yet I'm pulling teeth." If he didn't want to talk about this, he could have kept it to himself. The divorce was happening, so there was no point in admitting all of his transgressions.

"There were about a dozen instances."

I gave a slow nod, releasing a quiet chuckle because it was so ridiculous. "And I had no idea..." I gave another chuckle because I felt like an idiot. "If Cecilia hadn't told me, I wonder if I ever would have found out. Maybe when I got an STI..."

Adrien turned quiet.

"Why are you telling me all of this?"

The pause was endless, his eyes scanning the kitchen behind me, just a counter with a stove and a microwave next to a dishwasher and laundry machine, all condensed into a tiny space. "I just thought you should know."

I narrowed my eyes in suspicion. "How many times did I ask if there was anyone else—"

"I'm telling you now, Fleur. Leave it be."

"Leave it be." I shook my head. "So, were these relationships or...?"

"Not relationships. Just...hookups."

"Were you ever happy with me, Adrien?" I'd never let him watch me cry, and I wouldn't start now. But the tears started all the way down in my chest. I'd never felt so worthless.

"Of course I was," he said. "When I say they didn't mean anything to me, I'm telling you the truth."

"Then our sex was bad."

"That's not true either."

"Then it doesn't make sense, Adrien," I snapped. "Make it make sense."

"Beautiful women came on to me...and I struggled to say no. That's all there is to it." He gave a slight shake of his head.

"You do realize they only want to fuck you for your money, right?"

He released a heavy sigh.

"So this was all about ego? A pretty girl pumped you up, so you pumped into her?"

He wouldn't look at me.

"All those years I'll never get back..." He was threatened by my body count, but he'd exceeded that number during our marriage alone. There had been a moment, however brief it was, when I'd actually considered taking him back. But that was one woman, one time, a mistake. This was just objectively disrespectful. At least now, I didn't have to wonder if the marriage was salvageable. "Thanks for telling me...I guess."

He sat there and basked in the glow of his shame. He let the silence pass and intensify the pain that throbbed between us. "I know this is hard to believe, but my transgressions had nothing to do with my love for you. I regret all of it, regret it with all my heart. If I could take it all back, I would, because losing you has been the single most painful event of my life. I hate knowing you're here alone...while I sleep in the bed I used to share with you. There's been no one else since you've been gone, and I'll put my hand to the bible and swear to that."

I stared at the empty vase on my table, sculpted into a woman's derriere. I hadn't had time to put flowers in it.

"There are no more secrets. That's the whole truth. And I know it's crazy for me to even ask, but I would love another chance—"

A sarcastic chuckle escaped my lips as I rolled my eyes.

He hesitated, his eyes shifting to me. "I told you the truth, Fleur. You don't know how hard that was."

"Not nearly as hard as hearing it, I can tell you that much."

"I give you my word it won't happen again."

"Your word doesn't mean shit, Adrien. You promised to be faithful to me for the rest of our lives, and you shit all over that." Blue eyes popped into my mind, as they often did. A sexy stranger who occupied my nights and chased away my loneliness. He said he was a man of his word, and maybe I was an idiot for believing another man, but I believed him.

"I made a mistake—"

"Fuck up once, it's a mistake. Fuck up twice, it's a habit. Fuck up three times, and it's your character. You're a cheater, Adrien—that's who you are. You'll cheat on your next wife. And the next one..."

He succumbed to the silence, his head bowed like a dog that had received a smack on the nose.

"Cecilia saved me." I felt so much gratitude for the woman who'd fucked my husband. Whatever her intentions were, to drive me out of the house so she could take my place, I didn't really care. She'd told me the truth—and spared me. If I hadn't discovered this until a decade into the future, my youth would be gone, and I would have already had children with the man I now hated. "Saved my fucking ass."

Now that I knew the full truth, I didn't have to look back and wonder what I could have done differently. I didn't have to wonder if the marriage was worth saving, if perhaps I needed to grant mercy rather than rage.

But I also had to start over—to grieve all over again.

Paris was the most beautiful city in the world, but I didn't appreciate the flowers that grew on the balconies, the smell of fresh baguettes from the boulangeries, hot espresso on a cold morning, the beautiful people who met at outside cafés for a smoke and a drink. A part of me died when my marriage died.

And I wouldn't get her back.

Bastien texted me. *I'm in the neighborhood.*

I was so miserable I didn't even want to talk to my antidepressant. *I want to be alone right now*. He was always honest with me, straight to the point, so I decided to be the same back to him. If it were someone else, I wouldn't have bothered to text back, but I felt an inexplicable obligation toward him.

He didn't fire off questions or send me words of comfort. Didn't offer to come by or buy me a drink. He just let me be. *You know how to find me, sweetheart.*

Days passed. I went to work, came home, slept twelve hours a day because I had no ambition to be awake. Bastien didn't come by the bar or text me, so when I asked to be alone, he respected that request.

A part of me was afraid he thought I was giving him the brush-off, that he would find someone else whose company he preferred more than mine, and when I texted him again, he wouldn't text me back.

I still wasn't in the mood for companionship, but I didn't want to lose the one good thing I had in my life. ***I'm sorry I was harsh before***. It was three in the afternoon. I didn't know what he would be doing at that time, if he was still asleep or if he was out and about. The first time we'd slept together, he'd left early in the morning because he had a meeting. I wasn't sure what his schedule was like.

But his three dots were immediate—as always. ***You weren't.***

It was so easy to talk to him, strangely so. When I met Adrien, we were swept up in passion and laughter, and the whirlwind never stopped. I'd only known him for a year before we were married. With Bastien, the passion was tenfold, but the rest of the time, it was calm...and easy. Not that I should compare the two because I'd had a relationship with Adrien, and with Bastien, it was... something casual. ***Just didn't want you to think I was blowing you off.***

I'm too hot to blow off.

I wasn't sure if he was being playful or not, but I smiled anyway, hearing his voice in my head and picturing that handsome smirk. ***Very true.***

Hungry, sweetheart? I could go for a steak.

I hadn't eaten much the last few days, but talking to him had revved up my appetite out of nowhere. ***Yeah, that sounds good.***

I'll be there in fifteen minutes.

I quickly changed and put on makeup for the first time in days. I hadn't even worn it to the bar, and it had impacted my tips. No one wanted a depressed bartender who barely had the energy to get out of bed to show up for work.

I stepped outside in my coat, and at that moment, a blacked-out SUV pulled up on the one-way street outside the café. It came to a stop, and Bastien stepped out and opened the door for me, wearing dark jeans and a long-sleeved gray shirt, and the color really brought out the blue of his eyes. His towering height was more apparent against the vehicle because he stood taller than the roof. And his handsomeness was apparent too when he smiled like that, like I was the only person he wanted to see.

He stepped aside so I could move across to the other seat, and I felt his big palm give my ass a playful spank before he sat in the chair beside me and closed the door. The car took off before our safety belts were fastened.

He didn't make conversation, sat there with his elbow propped on the armrest, his fingers gently grazing the little bones in his jawline. When he felt my stare, he turned to meet my look. "Sweetheart?"

No man I'd been with had ever called me that before. Adrien never gave me a pet name. I imagined Bastien called a lot of women by the endearment, that it was a word he threw out to everyone, but I still felt warm when he called me that. "I forgot how hot you are."

His smirk widened, the smile reaching his pretty eyes. "Then you need to take a picture so you don't forget next time."

Traffic in Paris was the worst in the mornings and early afternoon when everyone got off work. It was so bad that it was better to walk or bike, which was what most people did. But even now in the evening, the roads were congested. The restaurant was only a few miles away, but it still took twenty minutes to get there.

The driver pulled up to *Le Relais de l'Entrecote,* and Bastien got out first before he helped me out of the SUV. There was a line of fifteen people standing outside waiting for a table, but Bastien walked through the double doors and straight to the hostess desk. He had a quick conversation with the woman in the black dress, saying something about someone named Luca, and then we were taken right to a table...and we got a lot of dirty looks.

We were given a table by the window, and Bastien pulled the table out so I could squeeze into the seat against the wall before he put the table back in place and sat down. It was a famous restaurant in Paris that served only one thing—steak and fries. You could order as many servings as you wanted, and waitresses in maid outfits came by and refilled the plates with a new piece of meat smothered in a sauce along with a new batch of fries. I'd been there once before, a couple years ago.

The waitress asked how we liked our steaks prepared before she fetched our drinks. Bastien ordered a stiff drink, as always, and I stuck to a glass of wine. Our food came as quick as our drinks, and the waitress piled our plates with meat and fries with a spoonful of gravy before she walked away.

Bastien cut into his meat and devoured his food like he hadn't eaten that day.

"Did you have a reservation?"

"No." He answered between bites, having manners despite his caveman attitude.

"Then how did you get a table so easily?"

"A friend of mine owns this place."

"Nice. I need to make better friends...like ones that work at Versace and Saint Laurent."

He gave a quick smile before he continued to eat.

I cut into my meat and felt my stomach clench because I was starving, the hunger pangs having been silenced by my broken heart for the last couple of days. I dipped my fries into the gravy, small and crispy, and then took another bite of my meat.

Bastien scarfed down his plate quickly, and the next time the waitress came by, she refilled his plate with another serving. It was like a buffet, except you didn't have to get up and grab food from a communal table.

"Did you skip lunch today?"

"No," he said. "Just hungry."

I finished my plate and considered another serving, but I knew I didn't need it. In a couple minutes, I would feel satiated. I wasn't packed with pounds of muscle like Bastien, so I couldn't eat all I wanted, even with the weight I'd lost over the past week.

He finished his second serving—and then ordered a third.

I shouldn't be aroused by a man's appetite, but there was something about his that got me going. The fact that he needed to eat thousands of calories a day because he had that much muscle to maintain, because he was strong enough to pick up a table and chuck it across the room like it weighed nothing.

I drank my wine, watched the cars pass on the road outside the window and tried not to stare at him too much because it felt rude. But he didn't seem to care that he was the only one eating. Didn't seem to care about anyone's opinion of anything, frankly.

I liked that about him.

He finished his plate then took a drink from his glass.

"Gonna go for a fourth?"

He smirked at my taunt. "I've had enough."

The waitress took our plates then left the dessert menu behind, which he didn't look at.

"I think your friend lost money tonight." He seemed to understand I was just teasing him rather than actually insulting him, so I continued with it.

He smiled even wider. "Good. He's an asshole."

"Your friend is an asshole?"

"They're all assholes."

"You know what they say, if everyone is an asshole, then you're probably the asshole."

"Oh, I'm definitely an asshole," he said. "But they're assholes too." He drank from his glass again, the ice cubes tilting with the angle of the glass. When it was empty, he returned it to the table and ordered another.

I was surprised he didn't ask how I was doing, why I'd gone dark for nearly a week, but that was something I liked about him. He never applied pressure to delicate matters. For a man, he had incredible intuition. For a man who could lift a car, he was awfully gentle when he needed to be. "How have you been?"

"Busy."

"With work?"

"I don't care for politics—but if you don't care for politics, you'll be governed by your inferiors."

"Are you involved in the day-to-day aspects of the Senate?"

"Sometimes. But right now, my time has been focused on finding someone who's always one step ahead of me."

"And who's that?"

"I told you trafficking is a problem, particularly in Paris."

"Yes, I remember."

"There's this asshole who has a whole enterprise centered around it."

185

"Then shouldn't he be easy to find?" I asked.

"No one wants to stick out their neck and snitch, which I get. If they snitch on him, then they can't be trusted not to snitch on others. And not to mention, they'll be hung and gutted for the transgression. He's managed to shut up an entire city, and he knows me well enough to avoid a confrontation."

"How does he know you well if you're enemies?"

His fingers rested on the top of his glass, and he gave it a quick shake before he took a drink. "It's a long story." Something in his tone suggested it was a story I would never hear, but he was nice enough not to ignore me or shut down the question entirely.

I hadn't known him very long, but I respected him like hell, respected him too much to pry. "Are you going to get a dessert?"

His mood was still slightly sour. "Sweets aren't my thing."

"Do you mind if I get something?"

A slow smile melted over his mouth, something about me getting something sweet bringing affection to his eyes. "Not at all, sweetheart." He placed the communal menu in front of me. "What are you thinking?"

I looked down at the list. "I love chocolate cake, but I've got a weak spot for profiteroles."

"Know how that goes..."

When the waitress came over, I ordered the pastry with a cup of coffee. "Thanks for letting me get something."

"I'm glad to see you eat."

"What does that mean?"

Instead of backpedaling or dropping his gaze, he kept his confidence. "You're a little thinner than the last time I saw you."

"You can tell?"

With his elbows on the table and his hands together, he looked at me head on. "I know your body. Know it very well." His eyes were so blue even in the dimly lit room, a man all the more handsome in his potent confidence.

The waitress interrupted the standoff when she brought the profiteroles and the coffee. Steam rose from the mug, and the plate was warm from the chocolate sauce they seemed to have just taken off the stove.

I sliced my fork into the layers of flaky dough then took a bite, all the flavors like a tide of warmth over my tongue.

He watched me eat the dessert, his eyes fully absorbed. "What do you think?"

"It's fucking good."

He smirked slightly before he drank from his glass again. "Women and their desserts..."

"Like men and their steaks."

He smiled again. "Touché."

I ate the entire plate of profiteroles and scraped up the little pieces left behind because my stomach had had an awakening. It was the first time I'd left the house for pleasure rather than for work. It was nice to do something other than mope. "Remember when I told you Adrien wanted to talk to me?"

He didn't answer or nod, just gave that hard stare.

I took that as a yes.

"Well, I found out what he wanted to tell me...that it was more than the one time." I'd kept this inside for almost a week, letting it rot my organs and bones until I was completely empty. "That there were at least a dozen different women. How I didn't get an STI, I'll never know."

He had no reaction to that, like he had suspected that all along or didn't want to fuel my raging fire with more fuel.

"I'm such a fool. I'm certain his older brother knew because they're close. I'm sure his best friend knew. I'm sure other people knew too, and they just didn't want to tell me. So there I was, walking around like a fucking idiot, oblivious to all of this."

"You aren't an idiot, sweetheart," he said gently. "We never suspect the people we trust. He's the fool for throwing away a damn good woman. I promise you he'll regret it for the rest of his life."

"He does seem apologetic—or I'm an idiot for believing his remorse."

"I have no doubt he regrets it," he said seriously. "And especially regrets getting caught."

I stirred my coffee because the cream had settled at the top. "He said he wanted to tell me the truth and, since he was honest with me when he didn't need to be, asked if there was a chance we could—"

An uncontrollable laugh escaped his lips as he crossed his arms over his chest.

My eyes shifted back and forth between his as I tried to understand what had just happened. "What?"

His laughs subsided, and he shook his head. "Nothing."

"What am I missing here?"

"Nothing," he repeated.

"Then you think my misery is funny?" I snapped.

"Not at all." He turned serious again. "I just think he's full of shit."

I continued to look at him, and for the first time, I felt deceit from him. Like there was something I was missing, but I couldn't put my finger on it. It wasn't a good feeling, and I didn't want to feel that way again. "I don't like this feeling."

"What feeling?"

"Like I'm the butt of a joke."

The seriousness in his eyes started to soften in remorse. "Sweetheart—"

"I would offer to pay for my meal, but now I need to storm out, so thanks for dinner." I shifted to the very edge of the table so I could squeeze through the tiny space between the window and the table.

He moved the table against the glass and cut off my escape. "Stop." He didn't raise his voice, not in the crowded restaurant where everyone was still oblivious to the rising conflict.

"I want to leave." I shifted the other way so I could squeeze between our table and the one next to us.

"I said, stop."

"Don't tell me to stop. Now, let me go."

He stared me down across the table before he shifted it over and let me pass.

I squeezed by, the occupants at the table beside us quiet when they felt our hostility. I walked out of the restaurant, my eyes on the ground, my face hot from the rage. It was too far to walk to my apartment, but I was broke, so I would have to use money I didn't have to waste to get out of there.

I made it outside, and the chilly air splashed onto my face like cold water. There wasn't a line of people anymore because it was almost midnight. I felt a little better when I was in the open air, when I wasn't across from the man who'd laughed at my stupidity, and I headed down the street in the direction of my apartment.

"Sweetheart."

I hadn't even heard him behind me, which seemed impossible when he was the size of a bear. I carried on like I didn't hear him, walking past the cars parked at the curb, the sidewalk empty of pedestrians.

"I'm talking to you."

"And I'm ignoring you."

He grabbed me by the arm and forced me to face him, using an amount of power that reminded me how small I was—and how strong he was. "You are not the butt of a joke." His hand went into my hair, and he fisted it like a leash. "*Ever.*"

I was paralyzed by those blue eyes for a moment, how hard and sincere they were. But then I snapped back to my anger. "You said you're an honest man, but then you sit there and laugh at me. You tell me it's nothing when I know it's not nothing, and you try to make me feel stupid—"

"I made him tell you."

I stilled when the revelation hit me right in the face. My eyes flicked back and forth between his as the embarrassment made my knees weak.

"I shouldn't have laughed—but I wasn't laughing at you. I just can't believe a man can be so dishonorable and cowardly. He told a lie so ridiculous I didn't know what else to do *but* laugh."

Still in shock at what he had said, all I could do was stare, my hair still in his closed fist, his arm around the small of my back like the bars of a cage.

"I will never lie to you." His grip loosened on my hair when he realized I wasn't going to run. "I'm sorry I made you feel otherwise." He cupped my face, his thumb on my cheek, caressing me like the first flower of spring.

"How—how long have you known?" I felt embarrassed that the man I was fucking knew more about my husband's infidelities than I did.

He continued to look me in the eye. "Awhile."

"Why didn't you just tell me?"

"Because it should come from him. Because he should look you in the eye—like a fucking man—and tell you what he did. Because it's a punishment for the crime that he committed, to feel like an asshole when he tells you what a piece of shit he is."

"How did you convince him to do it?"

"Convince isn't the word I would use." His eyes hardened as he looked at me, a hint of what he'd done to my ex-husband. "You deserved to know the truth. You deserved to know that you were never the problem. You deserved closure." He moved his hand back into my hair and gently pulled it from my face so he could see all of me. His arm tightened around me, and he pulled me closer into him, letting my cheek rest against his chest as he held me on the sidewalk, like he knew I needed a moment without his piercing stare.

He stood there for a long time, holding me in the light of the lamppost, the street quiet because we were the only ones there. His body produced enough heat to keep me warm even though it was a cold night, a perfect evening for a fire in a hearth. "Come home with me." He didn't state it like a question, but it still felt like one.

I pulled my face from his chest to meet his look. I felt like I'd been ripped to pieces by a pack of dogs, my heart on one side of the street and the rest of my entrails on the other. Someone I'd promised to love forever had done this to me, had hurt me, had humiliated me, and then he'd had the nerve to look me in the eye—and lie all over again.

But whenever I looked at those perfect blue eyes, I felt a calm river, an everlasting peace, a passion that muted all my other emotions. I felt more trust in a stranger than I did my own husband. I felt safe with someone I barely knew. I got swept up in his current and let it take me far out to sea. "Okay."

Chapter 12

Bastien

It was the first time she slept over and we didn't fuck.

She got into bed without taking off her makeup and snuggled into me, her leg hiked over my hip, her arm around my neck, using me as a body pillow. Sadness still throbbed in her eyes, and that was probably why she was able to drift off to sleep so easily.

My sleep schedule was all over the place and I wasn't tired, so I watched her for a while, the lights from the Eiffel Tower appearing in the crack between the curtains. At some point in her sleep, she turned the other way, facing her nightstand where her phone sat.

I left the bed and stepped into the sitting room, shutting the door behind me until it was just open a crack. I went to my desk and opened my laptop, going through emails and the mail that Gerard had left on the desk.

My phone lit up with a text message from Luca. *Heading to Crazy Horse.*

Again? It was a cabaret show similar to Moulin Rouge, more of a tourist spot than a local place.

I'm fucking one of the girls.

Then why do you want me to come?

Because there's a bar—and other girls.

I'll pass.

What's your deal, asshole?

I've already got a girl here.

So? She probably won't even notice you're gone.

I chuckled out loud. *Fuck you, Luca.*

Just get back before sunrise.

Take one of the other guys.

You know you're my boy.

Have fun, Luca.

His messages stopped.

I checked my emails then went through the mail on my desk. There was an invitation for the annual gala at Luxembourg Palace, another obligation to see one another as if we didn't see one another enough as it was. A black-tie event, one that I attended solo every year. I set it aside then went through the rest.

Luca texted me again. ***You still seeing that same girl? The married one?***

Yes.

He had no follow-up question to that.

I worked for a couple of hours, and when I finally felt tired enough, I returned to bed. She'd made her way to the center of the bed, curled up in the blankets like a fish caught in a net. I slid in beside her and did my best not to shift the mattress too much.

But it was enough, because her eyes opened, tired and dazed, and she looked at me for a long second, like this was a dream. Then her eyes filled with soft affection, like the sight of me brought inexplicable joy, and she moved into me like a child reunited with her favorite stuffed teddy bear.

I circled my arms around her and held her close, watching her use my shoulder as a pillow.

Her arm draped over my waist, and she tucked her leg between my knees before she released a sigh and fell right back into deep sleep.

I hadn't been tired a moment ago, but the sight of her at peace made my eyes grow heavy—and I fell asleep.

I was dead asleep when I felt it, a warm mouth around my dick.

A dream suddenly came to me, Fleur on her knees on the rug around my bed, trying to suck a dick that was far too big for her little mouth. My breathing changed, my body felt tight, and pleasure burned me from the inside out.

I automatically reached for her hair, my hand coming into contact with the softness that I had fisted countless times. I was aware of the warmth in the room, the sunlight through the crack in the curtains, the tightness in my balls.

My eyes found the strength to open, and I looked down to see her ass in the air, her mouth buried in my crotch. She grabbed my dick by the base to support its weight as she pushed her mouth over my length, barely making it past the halfway mark before she needed to withdraw to take a breath.

I propped my head up on my arm and watched her for a while, watched her eat my dick like a pancake breakfast.

Her eyes flicked up to look at me, mouth full of dick, that fine ass still in the air.

I wanted to come in her mouth, but she turned me on so much that it drove me insane, made me desperate to fuck her as hard as I could. I gripped the back of her head, and I forced her back, watching my dick slip from her lips and flop against my stomach. "Come here." Instead of directing her on top of me, I guided her beside me and shoved her face into the sheets. Her ass naturally popped up, and I moved behind her, my dick already slick from her tongue. I slipped inside her without resistance because she was more than ready for me.

She gave a cry when I shoved my full girth inside her, her screams muffled against the sheets because I continued to pin her neck down. I pounded into her like a whore from the brothel rather than a woman I actually cared for —and she seemed to like it. Her mascara bled onto the sheets, and her sharp nails dug into my knees from where she reached back and gripped me.

"You like that, sweetheart?" I fisted her hair and pushed her cheek to the sheets, her face turned so she could breathe. I usually gave her a fraction of my size, but this time, I gave it all to her, saw her wince through the pain, but she never protested. She took it like a champ—took it like it was her job.

"Yes...yes."

I continued to pound into her hard, never slowing my pace or having to edge myself, not when I was still partially asleep, my mind and body not fully connected. It allowed me to give it to her ruthlessly, harder than she anticipated.

Her hands started to flail, gripping the sheets and tugging them until they slipped off one of the corners. Her legs were wide open, but her pussy tightened over my dick with the grip of a viper—and she came with a scream.

I closed my eyes and savored the sound before I finished, giving her my seed when she squeezed it out of me, filling her pussy like it was the first time, even though it had been more times than I could count. Adrien had had this woman in his bed every night but chose to fuck around—the most idiotic thing I'd ever heard. But now my dick was the one plowing into her, and that was just fine with me.

I gave her ass a hard spank when I was finished, making her grunt in pain. I pulled out and spanked her again, hitting her so hard she rolled onto her side and moaned. The handprint was visible on her cheek, so I leaned down and kissed it, kissed the red, welted skin, made the pain feel good.

She softened at my kisses, turning her torso to watch me, her fingers moving into my short hair before she guided me toward her, bringing me over her so she could kiss me on the mouth. It was more than a quick kiss to start the day, but a long kiss with breath and tongue, like having my dick and my come wasn't enough for her, like she still wanted more—like all of me still wasn't enough.

I separated her knees then moved between her thighs, my hand deep in her hair as I kissed her, her body covered in the t-shirt she'd stolen from one of my drawers. I tugged it up to expose her tits before I sunk inside her again, feeling her suck in a breath against my mouth when she felt me, like she didn't just take me.

She must have been sore because she spoke against my lips. "Easy..."

I restrained myself from giving it all to her, invading her like she was a virgin, my rocking as gentle as the small waves at sunset.

Her ankles hooked together at the small of my back, and she kissed me as I moved inside her, her fingers deep in my hair, her other hand clawing at my back. "Yes...like that."

Dalia's Market, a run-down storefront in the 18th arrondissement, sat undisturbed under the lamppost, the street empty of cars, while the sidewalk held a camp of the homeless in tents, empty cups placed outside in the hope of donations—or a chance to con someone.

The blacked-out SUV pulled up to the front, while the others behind me came to a stop. The guys hopped out first, dressed in all black with masks over the bottom part of their faces, tactical vests covering their chests and backs. Armed with rifles, they fired at the latch on the rolled-down door until it popped free. Then they slid it up, revealing the stands of produce that would be available at dawn. They moved farther inside, unlocked the hidden door that led to the basement, and descended.

I stayed in the back seat and listened to the gunfire a moment later. It lasted for a couple seconds before it went quiet.

I took that as my cue and hopped out of the back seat, flanked by my two guys, as I headed down the stairs and saw the bloody sight below. Girls were huddled in the corner, latched on to one another and shaking like they were next to be executed. The tables contained bottles of over-the-counter medications, like ibuprofen and acetaminophen, but instead of finding those harmless drugs inside the containers, you'd find shit more sinister—and illegal.

I didn't care about the drugs—just the women forced to pack it.

There were dead men on the floor, brains splattered under the tables. I walked through the bodies, ignored the ones who trembled as their brains continued to troubleshoot their afflictions, and then found the three guys in the rear who had been kept alive. Their wrists were zip-tied behind their backs as they sat in the plastic chairs at the table, their cigars still burning where they'd been left behind.

One of my guys pulled out a chair for me then stepped away.

I took a seat, pulled out my own cigar, and lit up.

They put on their best poker faces, tried to be brave when they were about to shit themselves. One had already pissed himself. I could smell it. I took a puff as I stared at the first one. "Who's your supplier?"

He couldn't stop himself from shaking, knowing exactly who I was even though we'd never met. "We get the product from Jerome—"

"Not the drugs. The girls." I already knew who his supplier was, but I wanted to make an example out of him.

"I don't know," he said. "I just started here—"

I pulled out my pistol and shot him in the head. The sound of the blast was deafening in the enclosed space, even with the silencer on.

One of the other guys gave out an uncontrollable shout.

The other—the one who'd pissed himself—had wet eyes.

I turned to the next one. "Your turn." I aimed the gun at him.

This one didn't play games. "Godric." His eyes were down because he couldn't look at me, couldn't face down the barrel pointed at his head.

"Good," I said. "Where can I find him?"

"I—I don't know. I really don't know. You can ask the boss—"

"Who's the boss?"

"The man I work for...his name is Peter."

"Peter what?"

"Peter Astinoff."

I kept my gun on him. "Call him."

He hesitated, like he couldn't believe the request. "I—I don't have his number." He looked at his dead comrade. "He hired me—"

I pulled the trigger, and he fell out of the chair.

"*Please don't kill me.*" The man with the wet pants immediately started to beg for his life, trembling so hard in his chair that the tapping of the legs against the concrete was audible.

"Get me Peter, and you won't have to die in your own piss."

"I don't have his number, but I can get you to him."

"How?" I continued to hold the gun to his face.

"I think I know where he lives."

"You think?"

"He was having a party and wanted us to bring the girls... for entertainment."

I kept the gun trained on him, but for once, I was intrigued by this information. "Address?"

"I don't—don't know the address, but—but I remember how to get there." He could barely talk, afraid his brains were about to get blown across the floor. "It's the 4th arrondissement. I can take you there now."

I finally lowered the gun and nodded to one of my guys to cut him free.

When his wrists were unbound, he closed his eyes and released a heavy breath.

"Change your pants," I barked. "My car isn't going to smell like piss."

We drove across town to the 4th arrondissement, the roads empty at this hour. My witness was in a different car, a gun held to his temple. With the window cracked, I smoked a cigar, passing the old buildings and seeing Notre-Dame come into view, the cranes still in place because the renovation would take years.

Fleur texted me. ***You awake?***

I'd been simmering in the back seat, burning underneath my clothes. The women I'd liberated were being taken to a safe house by the guys. After they showered and changed their clothes, they would be given money and papers to head on their way or be reunited with the families from which they were stolen. Most of the girls weren't even legal adults yet. I wanted to ignore Fleur's message and let her think I was asleep because I was in a pissed-off mood, but I respected her too much to let her message go unanswered. **Working.**

She seemed to read my clipped tone because her response was brief. ***I'll talk to you later.***

I should just leave it at that because I had other priorities right now, but I couldn't. ***Are you okay, sweetheart?*** I was pissed as fuck right now, ready to burn down that house and force my enemies to breathe in the smoke, but all of that paused the second my concern for her grew.

Her three dots came right away. ***I'm fine. Just want you in my bed, is all.***

Normally, I would have smiled, but I felt nothing right now. ***Tomorrow.***

Okay, be safe.

Once I knew she was fine, I put my phone away and watched the line of cars pull up to a building behind an iron gate. It must be the place because my crew hopped out with the crowbar then proceeded to break down the gate with a couple swings.

I got out of the car as the guys formed a perimeter around the house, while the others carried the crowbar to the double front doors. They planned their coordinated attack in silence, and once the wordless cue was given, the attack happened simultaneously, the windows behind blown out with gunfire while the door was knocked down.

The men moved through the house, shooting down the security guys who had failed at their jobs. Blood splattered the walls, smoke bombs were thrown into hallways, screams were silenced by death. It happened quickly, framed family photos on the walls shattered by bullets.

I heard a woman's scream from upstairs, probably the wife or the mistress or the whore, who fucking knew.

I waited downstairs, listening to her scream as she was dragged into another room and then locked behind the door with her children. Minutes later, Peter was dragged down the stairs and to the center of the living room, forced on his knees like an execution.

"Wife and children are barricaded upstairs," one of the guys said as he approached me. "No injuries."

Peter's wrists were zip-tied behind his back. "Please don't hurt my family."

I walked up to him, stared hard into his frightened eyes, and then hit him in the face with my fist. "Insult me like that again and see what happens." I broke his nose, and blood splattered on me and the floor.

He dared not scream, but he breathed through the pain.

"You beg for your wife and your daughter, but you employ children whose mothers made the same plea." I squatted down before him so we were eye-to-eye. "How would you feel if I dragged your daughter down here and fucked her right in front of you? And all you could do was watch?"

He trembled at the words, both in terror and anger, his face turning beet red in an unexpressed rage. His eyes were locked on me like a rocket from a fighter jet.

"How would you feel if I made her work her hands bloody every day then locked her up every night? Sentenced her to a short life of manual labor that eventually broke her back? And she never saw the light of day again?"

He continued to shake, like he wanted to kill me for just saying those words.

"You're lucky I'm a better man than you are, because if I weren't, your wife would be my maid and your daughters would be my whores." I rose to my feet and stepped back before I pulled my pistol out of the back of my jeans. I cocked the gun before I pressed the end of the barrel right against his forehead. "It's simple. Tell me where I can find Godric, and you can walk upstairs and comfort your family."

His eyes closed as he felt the cool metal against his skin.

I waited for the answer I wanted, felt him tremble against the gun.

"Don't try my patience, Peter."

"I can't tell you."

"If you don't, your family will find you here—a bullet through the head."

"You may take my life—but Godric will take my entire family. He'll wipe out my bloodline. He'll hunt down my brothers and sisters and their families...my cousins in Albania. He'll execute my friends and their families and spit on them just for good measure. And only after that's done...when I have nothing to live for...he'll kill me." He stared at the floor, at my bloody boots. "I can't talk—and no one else will either."

The disappointment was like gasoline on my tongue, and the rage was a lit match. It was impossible to beat a man without ethics when I had to abide by my own. I chose to be the bigger man, but that made Godric the bigger opponent. There were lines I refused to cross, and Godric danced right over them. "As the first French Emperor of the Republic, I sentence you to death for violating *Homines ex codice* with the use of trafficked women as free and illegal labor." I fired the gun, and he fell back, blood pouring from the bullet hole in the center of his skull. "Rot in hell, asshole."

The SUV pulled up to the gate, and I checked in with security before I was granted permission to enter the grounds. I was escorted through the double doors, and then the butler invited me into the parlor. "Madame Dupont will be here shortly." He placed a tray on the coffee table, a pot of tea with floral teacups on saucers along with a platter of cranberry scones. He excused himself, leaving me alone in the room drenched in sunlight from all the open windows, the wallpaper a floral pattern, the chandelier made of crystal, the coffered ceilings restored and preserved.

I sat in the armchair and waited, looking out the window to the buildings beyond, dead tired behind the eyes but refusing to show it.

Then I heard the sound of her heels behind me, the gentle tap against the hardwood floor, the way the sound changed once she hit the custom rug her designer had selected for the space. I rose to my feet to greet her, wearing a gray collared shirt instead of my typical t-shirt out of respect.

She stopped before me, thin as a rail in a pink dress that reached past her knees, her blond hair elegantly done in soft curls, a necklace of sparkling diamonds around her throat. There were lines in the corners of her eyes and around her mouth, but other than the subtle signs of age, she'd been perfectly preserved in an eternal state of beauty. Her eyes filled with affection at the sight of me, as always. "My boy." She cupped my face in her hands, and she kissed me twice on each cheek.

I did the same to her. "You look beautiful, Mother."

"Thank you, son." She moved to the edge of the couch, and her butler stepped in to pour two cups of tea—even though she knew I didn't drink the piss.

Her butler excused himself, and we were left alone together.

With her ankles crossed like the Princess of Wales, she held her saucer and sipped her tea. The scones were left untouched because she hardly ate to remain as thin as she was. She only offered food to be polite. She returned the saucer to the table. "How are things, Bastien?"

I hated small talk. "The same. How's the country house coming along?"

"Ugh, one of the pipes broke, and there was a terrible flood. Delayed the renovation quite a bit."

"Sorry to hear that."

"There are worse things," she said. "So, are you seeing anyone?"

She always asked me this because she was interested in continuing the family line, not because she cared about my happiness. I didn't answer the question, not wanting to discuss my relationship with Fleur, not because I wanted to hide it—but protect it. "No."

"Bastien, you're in your thirties now—"

"I didn't come here to discuss how disappointing my personal life is."

Her hands came together on her knees, giving me that shrewd look packed with more intelligence than any person should have—especially your mother. "I know what you came here to discuss, and my answer hasn't changed."

I gave a slight shake of my head. "How can you protect him?"

"I don't protect him. I protect you both."

My temper flared right away, furious that I had to have this conversation for the millionth time. "He's vile—and you fucking know it."

She didn't react to my rage. Didn't react when one of her guards stepped into the room to check on her well-being. Her eyes moved to him, and she gave a slight nod to dismiss him. As if I would ever hurt my mother. "Tell me where he is."

She held my gaze with the stillness of a statue. She answered my question with silence.

"How can you possibly support someone like him?"

"I never said I did."

"Then support me, and tell me where the fuck he is."

She gave a slight shake of her head. "When you become a parent, you sign a contract with infinite terms and agreements. And those terms and agreements bind you to love your child unconditionally, whether they become the president of France or take a seat on murderers' row. It doesn't matter whether I agree or disagree with his actions or yours. I love you both with all my heart. I will not betray him—and I will not betray you either."

"Has he asked you how to find me?"

"No." She didn't blink, didn't react to the question, like it was the truth. "You're the one who seeks him, not the other way around. You have differences that can't be resolved. As much as I'd like to have my sons under the same roof on Christmas, I understand that's simply not possible. If you can't come to an agreement, then live in peace—separately."

"He traffics innocent women." I did my best to keep my voice low, but my anger seeped out. "Do you understand that? Most of these girls aren't even seventeen years old. *They're fucking children.* Based on their appearance, they're either sent to whorehouses or sent to work assembling guns or packing drugs. This is your city, the greatest city on earth. And this is how you want your city to operate? We're the City of Light, not the City of Darkness."

She had no reaction to that, her face straight and her eyes dead.

"You have nothing to say?" I snapped.

She blinked, and that was it.

I sat back in the armchair and sighed as I dragged my hand down my face, the frustration burning the tips of my fingers. My mother was the one connection I had to him, but I couldn't force her to surrender information, and not just to abide by the code. "Then I ask you to arrange a meeting with the two of us. No guns. No men."

She continued her hard stare, having a better poker face than any man.

"Just a conversation."

She took a breath and let it out slowly, her long hair behind her shoulders.

"You know I'm a man of my word. I would never bring violence into your home."

She broke eye contact and looked at the fireplace.

"You're the only person he respects. If you asked him to come under the banner of truce, we would abide by it."

She considered it for a long time, her eyes glued to the fireplace.

I'd searched the streets for him. I'd tortured people for information, but they were a hell of a lot more afraid of him than me. Unless I found where he was and took him myself, I would never get what I wanted. My mother was the only connection I had to my brother.

She finally turned back to me after careful consideration. "I'll ask Godric to consider it—but that's the most I can do."

Chapter 13

Fleur

Bastien didn't text me.

He said I would see him tomorrow, but tomorrow was today, and there was no sign of him. I didn't text him because I didn't want to smother him with my neediness. It was a casual relationship and he didn't owe me anything, but his silence made me wonder if his flame for me had been extinguished. He said his longest fling was a week, and we'd been going at it for a month now. So I assumed that he would pull the plug any day, that he would get tired of me when he found my replacement on his midnight adventures.

I didn't want it to end, not yet, but holding on to him tighter would just push him away quicker.

So I didn't text him.

I was alone in my apartment with the TV on, the darkness pressing against the windows while it rained. An ambulance drove by, and the sound reverberated against the buildings as it passed and then faded as it crossed the bridge. The divorce papers were on the dining table because I would submit the paperwork tomorrow.

I didn't have a shift at the bar tonight, but I wished I did just to stay busy. I knew I needed to find a job better than that one, something that paid enough for me to start a new life. I grabbed my laptop and searched job listings in the hope I would find something that paid well and that I was remotely qualified for.

But it was slim pickings.

Bastien texted me. ***I've got a lot on my mind right now. I'll talk to you tomorrow.***

I was relieved and disappointed by that message. When I asked for space, he gave it to me without an interrogation, so I did the same for him. Most guys would have just left me hanging, and then if I asked about his silence later, he would have called me clingy or annoying. But Bastien didn't do that. He was different. He treated me like I was important even though I was someone whose name he would forget in a couple months. If he settled down someday, whoever he gave his heart to would be the luckiest woman in the world. ***You know where to find me.***

I went to the courthouse the next day and submitted the finalized paperwork. Once it was processed, the divorce proceedings would move to a hearing. Adrien had earned most of his wealth while he was married to me, so we had to settle all the communal property, from the house in Paris to the one we owned in the Loire Valley.

But I didn't want any of it.

After that, I went on a few job interviews I'd set up, but I could tell by their reception of me that I had no chance of getting the positions. One was for a clerk at the courthouse, another was for an assistant at an art house, and another was an office job for an investment company.

By the time I made it back home, it was evening and time for dinner, but I had no food in the apartment. I decided to head downstairs to Poppy Café to order some fondue fries and have a smoke, sitting alone while groups of friends met up together after a day at the office, having a drink and a smoke before heading home to their apartments.

Bastien texted me. *I'm in the neighborhood.*

My heart did a little dance inside my chest, and that gave me a jolt of fear. When did my happiness become so dependent on this man? When did I become so attached? I should be heartbroken over Adrien, and despite what he did, I should still miss him. But now, all my thoughts were occupied by the man who'd picked me up in a bar. *I'm having a smoke at Poppy Café.*

Sounds like you had a rough day.

You could say that...

See you in a sec, sweetheart.

The black SUV appeared a moment later, and the behemoth of a man appeared. In a long-sleeved black shirt and dark jeans with boots, he approached my table on the patio, drawing attention from the other women seated nearby and the pedestrians who walked down the cobblestone street toward the mall. He did something he'd never done before—and leaned down and kissed me.

I saw cold stars and felt hot flames on my lips. A surge of affection that started in my core made it to my throat and my heart. The attachment I feared had just increased tenfold.

He took the seat across from me and pulled out a cigar before he lit up. Nonchalant, he got the attention of the waitress and ordered one of his stiff drinks, oblivious to the mark he'd left on my mouth—and my heart.

He took a drink before he took a puff of his cigar. The smoke rested on his tongue for a long time before he released it through his mouth, creating a big cloud of smoke around us. He crossed his arms over his chest, the cigar resting between his fingertips, and he stared at me for a solid five seconds.

I knew he wanted to know about my day but didn't want to pry. "I submitted the paperwork—for the last time, I hope."

"It will be."

"I guess it feels different this time because I know it'll go through."

"Isn't that a good thing?"

"I'm happy to be free of Adrien, but it's the first time I've truly realized that I'm getting divorced. I'm going to court and everything. Going to take back my maiden name. I was so busy being angry that I forgot what would come afterward."

He watched me for a while, his arms still crossed over his chest. "You're scared."

"I'm not scared. I just... It's hard to start over." I'd lost most of my friends. I loved his parents, but now they would never speak to me again, even though I was the victim in the marriage. I loved his entire family, felt like they were my family, and now I would never see them again. It fucking sucked.

"It's okay to be scared, sweetheart. You can't be brave if you aren't scared—and you are brave."

All the pain I felt was replaced by warmth, warmth that he put there. "How do you do that?"

"What?" He cocked his head slightly.

"You always know what to say."

He gave a slight shrug. "I don't bullshit, so you know I mean everything I say."

"Maybe..." Maybe it was because I could trust him. He was the only person in my life I had to trust.

He took another puff of his cigar before he kept it in his mouth, let the taste absorb into his tongue. He let the smoke out from the crack between his lips.

I finished my cigarette and put it out, knowing I needed to stop the habit again. It'd gotten worse over the last few weeks. When I thought Bastien was trying to shake me, it got worse, going from one cigarette a day to at least five. "I had a couple job interviews. I didn't get any of them."

"They answered you that quickly?"

"No, but I could tell they weren't interested. I wasn't qualified for most of the jobs, so I'm not sure why they interviewed me in the first place."

"What kind of work are you looking for?"

I shrugged. "Anything with decent pay, really. I'm tired of working nights too. Hard to believe, but I used to be a morning person before I started at Silencio."

"Are you decent with computers? Spreadsheets, Excel, shit like that?"

"I suppose." I owned a laptop, but I didn't use it much. Had never worked in an office before. "I'm a fast learner, whatever is thrown at me."

"I can get you a position at one of my investment firms. One of my finance guys needs an executive assistant— and he's gay."

"What does that have to do with anything?"

He smirked. "You think I'm gonna let my girl work for some asshole, wearing a tight pencil skirt all day? That ass is mine." He took another puff of his cigar, and when he spoke, the smoke billowed out of his mouth. "It's yours if you want it."

"Your girl?" I asked without thinking, surprised that he'd said that.

He rested the cigar between his relaxed fingertips, lounging in the chair like he wasn't the least bit stressed about the label he'd used so effortlessly. "I said what I said." With confidence in his stare, he looked at me like he didn't care how I felt about that. He didn't give a damn what anyone thought of him, and that included me. "So?"

His words made my heart race in excitement, made my palms warm despite the cold night air. But it also made the fear worse, because the last thing I wanted was to be in the same position as the one I'd just left. "That's really sweet of you to do that, but it wouldn't be right."

"How so?"

"I would be taking the job from someone actually qualified for it."

"Let me give you a life lesson, sweetheart. When someone opens a door, you just walk through it. Don't wait for it to close because it might be locked the next time you try to open it. Life is fucking hard, and you should use every advantage you have at your disposal. The advantage you have right now is me. Use me."

Every moment I spent with him made me more attracted to him. The words he spoke, the confidence he showed, the straightforward, no-bullshit way he handled his life and everyone in it. The pull between us grew in intensity and had the strength of a black hole, sucking me further into his soul. I'd loved Adrien with all my heart and wanted to spend my life with him, but I'd never felt for him the way I felt for Bastien, a man I still considered a stranger in a lot of ways. I didn't know how to process these feelings. I didn't know if I should see it through or pull the plug while I still had the strength.

"I'll tell him you'll be there on Monday." He tapped his cigar into the ashtray and let the ashes sprinkle the bowl before he took another puff, his jawline sharpening when he pulled the smoke into his mouth.

I was desperate for a job, desperate to be out of that bar where all the sleazebags hit on me all night long. I wanted to be in bed at a reasonable hour, not at four a.m., not unless I was with Bastien. "Thank you."

He enjoyed his cigar in silence, looking at me across the table with his arms crossed.

"So...how have you been?" I knew he'd had a rough few days, judging by his clipped tone over text. He was usually playful whenever we spoke, and when he wasn't, I knew something else was on his mind.

"Bunch of bullshit at work."

I didn't ask for specifics. If he wanted to share, he could.

"Some of my dealers continue to use trafficked women as free labor. I took down one of them, but he refused to roll on his supplier."

"Roll?"

"Snitch," he explained. "The guy has two teenage daughters too. How fucking sick is that?"

"What did you do?"

"He broke the law, so I had to execute him."

"Even though he has a family?"

"I don't give a shit if you have a family or not," he snapped. "You want to deal in my city, then you follow the rules. That fucking simple." He put out the cigar then grabbed the drink instead.

"I didn't mean to offend you."

"If you don't want to offend me, then don't judge me." Now his eyes were ruthless, and for the first time, they were ruthless for me.

"I wasn't judging you," I said calmly. "I'm sorry if I made it seem that way."

His eyes flicked away and he took a breath, an attempt to calm himself. "I have to maintain order. If I let a family man live, then I have to let another man live. Then I'll lose respect and authority, then the Republic will fall, the old order will return, and Godric will rule this city. Trust me, no one wants that—even if you aren't in the game."

I didn't know what to say to that. I was afraid if I said anything else, I would provoke him again. "I missed you these last few days—and the last thing I want to do is upset you. So please forget I said anything." I didn't like his angry side. I loved his intense and playful side, the way he smiled when I complimented him, the way he smothered me in his affection even when he didn't touch me.

Slowly, his anger passed like a storm cloud moving over the sky. Light came back into his eyes like the rising sun. He raised his hand slightly and gestured for the check. "My place or yours?"

"Yours." My apartment was small, the walls were slanted and restrictive for a man his height, and it was messy and cold. I loved his home, loved the soft sheets on his bed, his enormous bathroom with an expansive vanity, the view of the Eiffel Tower from the window of the terrace. I loved the large fireplace in the sitting room, the way it warmed my naked body when we fucked on the couch.

When the tab came, he slipped a wad of cash inside, way too much for the drinks and fries we'd ordered, and then he pulled out his phone and fired off a message to his driver. "Let's go, sweetheart."

When we walked into his bedroom, he pulled his shirt over his head, revealing a rock-hard chest and stomach covered in black ink. His shoulders were like mountains, and his biceps looked like grenades.

He came at me with that look that could kill before he pulled my sweater over my head and unclasped my bra. He lifted me into him so he could smother me in kisses, kissing my shoulder then my collarbone, kissing the hollow of my throat then my chest. He carried me to the edge of the bed and dropped me on it before he moved for my boots and jeans, tugging everything off, taking my thong with the jeans.

He grabbed my ankles and placed my feet against his chest before he dropped his jeans and boxers, letting them fall to his knees before he grabbed my hips and tugged my ass to the edge. He moved in a rush, like it was the first time he had me, the first time he got to bury himself inside me and release. He folded my knees against my waist then pushed inside with a satisfied sigh. "Fuck, I missed this pussy." He grabbed one of my tits and squeezed hard as he started to thrust inside me, my ass over the edge, giving me his full length like he wanted it to hurt.

I reached out my hands for his hips, and I tried to grip them to pull myself back into him. It'd been days of separation but it felt like weeks, and having him inside me felt so damn good, no matter how much it hurt. It was like a glass of cool water on a hot day. A warm meal on a winter night. Exactly what my body needed to feel good.

His hand left my tit and went for my throat. He squeezed it as he fucked me, one hand still pinned underneath my thigh, folding me like a pretzel because I was flexible enough to bend the way he wanted.

Once he started, he didn't let up, like he wanted to fuck me into a fast climax because he was eager to come. His handsome face tinted red, and the cords started to pop in his neck and his forearm. "Play with yourself."

My nails continued to dig into his hips as I held on, his dick even fuller at this direct angle, filling me up completely. Watching him work and thrust to fuck me was enough to make me come, and I was already at the threshold.

"Show me." He squeezed my throat.

My fingers went to my clit, and I started to play with myself, rubbing in a circular motion, applying the pressure that I liked. I tried to gasp, but he tightened his grip and my words disappeared into the void.

Less than a minute later, I finished, bucking against my fingers, his big dick ballooning inside me even more as he watched me reach the clouds.

He grabbed on to my hips and tugged me hard against him, giving me all his length as he came, as he released deep inside me and made one of his biggest deposits. He gave the sexiest moan when he finished, his eyes locked on me possessively. "Turn over."

Lost in the haze of the lingering climax, I didn't understand what he said.

"I said, turn over." He pulled out and started to roll me over, getting me on my hands and knees. He grabbed my hips and tugged me to the edge of the bed again before he shoved himself inside me once more, just as hard as he'd been a minute ago. He fisted my hair and tugged me back like I was a horse, and he fucked me relentlessly. Then his palm struck my ass with a hard smack.

I cried out then moaned, hating the pain but loving the pleasure that followed.

He spanked me again, harder this time.

I cried out louder, feeling the sting of his palm against my flesh, feeling how hot and red the skin turned.

"Want me to stop, sweetheart?" His palm turned gentle, his fingers kneading my ass as he continued to fuck me.

"No."

His fingers grazed over the flesh gently before he gave me another squeeze. Then he spanked me again, harder than before. "I didn't think so."

I woke up in the middle of the night to pee.

That was when I realized he wasn't there. The sheets were cool, like he'd been gone awhile, like he hadn't left for a moment to use the bathroom. I blinked a couple times to discern the darkness in the bedroom before I left the bed. I'd fallen asleep without any clothing, so I helped myself to a t-shirt from one of his drawers. My fingers grazed something cool, and that's when I realized there was a pistol there. I stilled before I gently removed the shirt without touching the gun and pulled it over my head, the soft cotton immediately swallowing me whole like a blanket. I went into his big bathroom with the golden sinks and the dark wallpaper and did my business in the dim light. When I left, I looked through the crack in the door that led to the sitting room and found him sitting at his desk, the fire burning in the hearth and basking him in a gentle glow, his eyes out the window on the Eiffel Tower and the rest of the city.

I watched him for a while, seeing the heaviness in his eyes, the weight of his troubles.

He brought a cigar to his lips and took a drag as he continued to stare out the window. After a pause of several seconds, he released the smoke from his mouth, creating a cloud that hung in the room before it floated elsewhere.

I opened the door wider and stepped into the room.

His eyes immediately flicked to me like he didn't realize I was awake. He immediately ground the tip of the cigar in the black ashtray on his desk to put it out. His striking blue eyes looked into mine with that usual calm confidence, a man who was always composed, regardless of what transpired underneath. "A little early for pancakes..."

The shirt was so big that one side of it slid off my body and exposed my shoulder. It almost hit my knees, fitting like a dress rather than a shirt. "It's never too early for pancakes." I gave him a slight smile before I approached his desk, my arms across my stomach because there was a cold draft in the room from where he cracked the balcony door to let the smoke out.

He left his chair and wordlessly shut the door, stopping the cold air from entering the room. He didn't move behind the desk again but instead came straight to me, circling his arm around the small of my back and pulling me into him hard before he brushed a kiss over the corner of my mouth. "Go back to bed, sweetheart." He was warm to the touch, hot like the fire that burned in the hearth, bare-chested and covered in his black ink. His black sweatpants hung low on his hips, and he was barefoot.

"What about you?" I asked quietly.

"Not tired." He leaned against his desk and crossed his arms over his large chest, his eyes showing the fatigue he claimed not to have.

"Something is bothering you." As far as I knew, he was always beside me all throughout the night, whether he was awake or not. But something troubled him enough to get out of bed and stay there.

His blue eyes were locked on mine with that quiet confidence. "I knew what I signed up for when I took this job. It is what it is."

"I'm sure you'll find him."

"That'll be the easy part." His eyes shifted past me, back out the window with the Eiffel Tower brilliant in the dark.

"What does that mean?" I asked.

He was quiet for a long time, letting the silence pass for so long it seemed like he might not say anything at all. "My job isn't usually complicated, but in this case, it is."

"Why?"

He gave a slight shake of his head before he looked at me again. "These are my problems, not yours."

"I care about your problems the way you care about mine." A cheating husband and an impending divorce were probably inconsequential compared to the stuff he had to take on, but he still seemed invested in my well-being—and I was invested in his.

He dismissed what I said with his silence. "Are you busy next Saturday night?"

"I think I have a shift at the bar."

"You have a new job, remember?"

"Oh yeah... But I still need to put in my two-week notice—"

"You don't owe them shit. They'll get another pretty girl to take your spot in a day."

I still felt bad about taking the handout, but it wasn't like I was taking cash straight out of his wallet. I needed to move on and rebuild the life that had been taken from me. "Why are you asking?"

He reached for a card on his desk, a champagne-pink invitation with gold writing. "I've got this gala at Luxembourg Palace. I'd like you to come with me." He tossed it back on the desk.

"Do you normally bring a date to these things?" He didn't seem like the kind of guy to attend parties in the first place, a man who lurked in the shadows with a gun tucked into his jacket.

"No."

"It doesn't seem like your scene."

"It's part of the job."

"If you don't normally bring a date, then why are you asking me?"

"Because I want you to come with me." He cocked his head slightly as he looked at me. "Is that a problem?"

I stilled at the power in his stare, the way he made me freeze with those blue eyes. "No."

"Then it's settled."

"Is this a black-tie type of thing?" I had been broke since the moment I'd moved out. The money I earned went to rent and food. I spent everything I made, and it wasn't unusual for me to have twenty euros in my account until my next check came in. Thankfully, Bastien offered to pay for everything when we were together because I couldn't even afford a drink most of the time. But a fancy party like this required a gown and diamonds and designer heels—all of which I didn't have.

"Yes."

I gave a slow nod, unsure how to handle this. "I appreciate the invitation, but I don't think I can make it—"

"Cut the shit and be straight with me. I'm inviting you to a party, and you're acting like I've got a gun to your head. Do I bullshit with you?"

Stuck in the headlights of his stare, I just stood there.

"Answer the question."

"No."

"Then don't bullshit with me." He didn't raise his voice, but he managed to be absolutely terrifying anyway.

"I don't want to make it awkward, but...I just can't afford that right now."

His eyes narrowed like he didn't understand.

"I can't buy a dress or heels right now. I know how these parties are, and I don't have the means. I have stuff back at the house, but if I try to get it before the divorce, Adrien will be vindictive and stop me because he'll know I'll be using the stuff with you. And the last thing I want is for you to buy me anything—"

"I'm your man. I'll buy you whatever the fuck I want."

A flush entered my cheeks, warmth and terror mixing together to form a cyclone in my heart. Never in my life had I been so scared of a single man, scared of the power that burned right at his fingertips. "That's the second time you've said something like that."

"Like what?"

"That this is more than casual."

His blue eyes were locked on my face with a hint of viciousness. It was just a stare, but it was threatening, like he was sizing up an opponent rather than looking at the woman he was bedding.

My voice trembled from that ferocious stare. "Look...I'm not looking for anything serious right now. I moved out of my husband's house two months ago. I'm not even divorced yet. I'm in no place to be anything more than… casual."

He continued his ruthless stare, not blinking once since this topic had been broached. His arms remained crossed over his hard chest, the biceps of his arms enormous bulges under his dark ink. He didn't say a word, but his silence was loud enough to be present in the conversation.

"I just…want to make that clear." From the first time I'd seen Bastien, it'd been a whirlwind of passionate nights and heated kisses and ass-grabs. It was exactly what I needed right now, but I didn't want anything more, not when my heart was still broken, not when I couldn't imagine giving my heart to another man after what Adrien had done to me.

His head remained cocked and his eyes intense.

I waited for him to say something, and I swallowed the tension down my throat.

He continued to look at me, his thoughts a mystery, his reaction restrained. "Okay."

"I can't see myself in a relationship for a very long time."

"Okay."

Something about the way he spoke made it seem like his words were hollow, like they were meaningless. "What does that mean?"

"I said okay."

"But the way you're saying it... It's like you're dismissing me."

He continued his hard stare.

"You mean a lot to me, and I don't want to mislead you."

"Okay."

"You're doing it again. It's like you don't believe me—"

"He hurt you. I get it," he said. "You need time."

He seemed to accept what I said, said what I wanted to hear, but there was something to his tone, to his stare, that made me feel otherwise. Like my words made no difference whatsoever.

He pushed off the desk and walked around it to open one of the drawers. He grabbed a wad of cash rolled up in a rubber band and set it at the edge of the desk. "Buy whatever you need."

The top denomination was a five-hundred-euro bill and there had to be at least twenty bills in the roll, so it must have been about ten thousand euros—just sitting in one of the drawers in his desk. Not even locked up in a safe. "I can't take your money."

He stared me down, a slight look of annoyance in his gaze. "You can take the money and save me a shopping trip—or you can be stubborn and waste my time."

My eyes shifted away when I couldn't handle that stare.

He took the wad of cash off the table and walked over to where my purse sat on the armchair. He dropped the money inside then headed back to the bedroom, a muscular behemoth who made the floorboards creak under his weight. "Let's go to bed, sweetheart."

When I woke up the next morning, he was already out of bed.

I checked the time on my phone and saw that it was noon.

I left the bed, used the restroom, and then found him in the sitting room, already dressed for the day like he'd completed his workout and showered while I slept like a baby. He was in an olive-green long-sleeved shirt and black jeans and boots—fucking delicious as usual.

"Morning, sweetheart." He sat at the dining table, drinking a cup of coffee while reading the newspaper. He patted his thigh for me to take a seat.

I smiled then dropped onto his lap, circling my arm around his neck before I kissed him. My shirt rose up my thighs, and his fingers grazed over the bare skin that was exposed. "Morning."

"Hungry?"

"Assume I'm always hungry until told otherwise."

He smirked, the morning light making his blue eyes shine. "I want to show you my favorite spot."

"I find it hard to believe there are better pancakes out there."

"You'll have to be the judge of that."

I got dressed and did what I could with my hair. My makeup had turned into a mess, so I washed it off and chose to have a clean face instead. I wondered if I should pack a bag whenever I came over here, but that felt too serious when I'd just told him I only wanted casual. Dressed in the clothes I wore yesterday, his driver took us to the restaurant in the 10th arrondissement and pulled up to the curb.

I read the sign out front. "Holybelly. I think I've heard of this place."

"It's an American breakfast joint." He got out first and held the door open for me. "The French do everything better—eat, drink, fuck—except breakfast. The Americans take the gold for that." He led the way, entered the restaurant first, and grabbed us a booth.

The place was packed with people. Not a single table was empty. I sat across from him, a bit self-conscious that I didn't have any makeup on. It was different when it was just the two of us in bed or at his dining table. But in public, I felt like a slob. At least I'd brushed my teeth with his toothbrush. When he saw me do it, he just smirked and continued whatever he was doing.

He seemed to notice my mood because he asked, "Something wrong?"

"It's nothing." I grabbed the menu and looked at the options. They had a sweet stack, pancakes topped with fruit and their homemade whipped cream, and they had a savory stack, pancakes topped with fried eggs and bacon. Everything looked good.

"Sweetheart." He didn't raise his voice, just changed his tone.

My eyes flicked up to his, seeing his hard stare. "I feel a little weird without makeup on..." I always wore makeup when I left the house unless I was depressed. When Adrien and I first separated, I didn't have the drive to put any effort into my appearance.

"Why?" He cocked his head slightly.

"I just...look better when it's on."

"I'd fuck you either way." He sat forward, his elbows on the table as if he didn't need to look at the menu. He gave me that same intense stare that he did from the other side of the bar, eye-fucking me right on the spot.

The waiter came over and took our drink order. I got a coffee and Bastien did too.

We were left alone again, the tension still there even though the conversation had died away.

"Is this where you usually bring your girls?"

"My girls?" he asked.

"You know, the girls who stay until the next morning."

He smirked like I'd told a joke rather than asked a serious question. "No. I come here with the boys."

"You come to brunch...with a bunch of guys."

"Why is that hard to believe?"

"Brunch is a girl thing, isn't it?"

"Good food is good food. We usually meet up once a week, on Sundays. Talk shop."

"That's pretty cute."

"Cute?" he asked.

"A bunch of guys meeting up on Sundays for pancakes. Pretty cute."

He smirked again, his stare lingering on my face. "Don't get any ideas."

"What kind of ideas could I get?"

"I don't do threesomes with men."

"That's not at all the idea I had," I said with a chuckle. "I'm not interested in threesomes either, especially when I have you."

His smile faded, and he gave me that hard look that had become his signature stare.

The waiter returned to our table to take our order, his long, curly hair pulled back in a bun.

"I'll do the savory stack," Bastien said. "She'll take the sweet stack with a side of eggs and the baked beans."

"You got it, Bastien." The guy took the menus and walked off.

"Did you just order for me?" I asked.

"Trust me, sweetheart." He took a drink from his coffee, his elbows on the table, the sunlight coming through the window behind me and striking his handsome face. Then he returned to his favorite pastime and stared at me like I wasn't a person, but a painting on the wall.

I watched the people in the restaurant for a while, and when I looked back at him, his stare was still on my face. He was comfortable in the silence, content just sitting there with me like we'd known each other forever rather than the blink of an eye. "What's the gala for?"

"Networking."

"Doesn't the Senate see each other all the time?"

"Not necessarily. President Martin will be there as well."

"As in, the president of France?"

"Yes."

"You know him?"

"Oh, I definitely know him."

I didn't get starstruck and I didn't think of the president as a celebrity, but I had no idea what I would say to him if I met him. Didn't follow politics. Barely understood the parameters of the Senate. I was too busy with my own shit to care about law and legislature. "I'm surprised they want to socialize with you publicly."

"You know what they say...hide in plain sight. You could look corruption in the eye and have no idea it's corruption's gaze you meet. The public interacts with my world on a daily basis, but they're none the wiser."

"That's a scary thought."

"It's our job to govern our citizens. It's also our job to protect them. I like to think we do both—and make something for ourselves in the process. Instead of spending tax dollars sending the police after criminals they can't possibly arrest, it makes more sense to profit from it. And those tax dollars go back to the citizens."

"Well, some of it does."

A slow smirk moved over his lips. "Yes. Some."

"Do you pay taxes?"

"Not from the tariffs I collect. But I pay taxes on the revenue earned from my businesses, like the investment company."

"How many businesses do you own?"

"Many."

I understood his wealth and his power, but I didn't understand how someone so young could have accomplished so much. "How old are you?"

"Thirty-three." He didn't ask the question in return, either because he already knew or because he didn't care.

"That's a lot to accomplish in thirty-three years."

"Well, I've been in the game for a long time."

"Ten years?" I asked. "That's still not that long." If he'd started in his early twenties, he was probably too young and immature to seem like a real threat to other men.

"It's been more than ten years," he said quietly. "It's been my whole life."

There was so much packed in those words, an epic tale I would probably never hear.

"Authoritarianism, rulership, power...it all runs in my veins." His eyes flicked past me to the door, and that hard expression slowly softened like he recognized someone who just walked inside. "What a pleasant surprise."

Two guys approached our table, both looking at Bastien like they knew exactly who he was. "You come here without us now?" The guy was tall with dark hair, fit and muscular like Bastien and just as arrogant. "I see how it is."

"I don't remember getting an invitation from you," Bastien fired back.

"We were in the neighborhood," the other one said, a tanned guy with jet-black hair. "And we were hungry."

The first one looked at me, and after a long stare, he looked at Bastien—full of accusation.

"Luca, this is Fleur." He nodded toward me.

Luca gave me a nod. "I've heard nothing but good things. Very good things..."

Bastien ignored him and introduced the other guy. "Gabriel."

"Nice to meet you both," I said, a little intimidated by these two equally strong and attractive men.

"Since you've got a booth, and we aren't waiting fifteen minutes for a table—" Luca moved to my side of the booth to take a seat "—we'll join you."

Bastien snapped his fingers. "Get your ass up. You aren't sitting next to my girl."

He did it again—called me his girl.

Luca raised both hands in a form of surrender and left the booth.

Bastien took his place, sliding into the spot next to me and dropping his arm over the back of the booth on top of my shoulders.

The two guys slid into the leather seat across from us.

There was an awkward pause, both of them looking at me like they'd never seen a woman before.

I grabbed my coffee and took a drink.

Bastien broke the tension. "How'd it go last night?"

"Squealed like a pig," Luca said. "Like they all do."

"Hector Turner is the one who closed down the port," Gabriel said. "People are saying he lost his mind because someone murdered his daughter, and he refused to let business resume until they found the killer. He wanted to put a target on the killer's back, but he just put the target on himself."

I had no idea what they were talking about, but they spoke freely in front of me, like I would never talk or I was deemed trustworthy.

"Heard about Peter," Luca said. "His family put the house on the market and fled for Albania."

"Good," Bastien said. "They aren't welcome in my city."

"Martin is gonna snap," Luca said. "I hear his collar is getting tighter by the day."

"This city ain't that big," Gabriel said. "Especially for someone as big as Godric. He's gotta be somewhere—"

"Then why don't you find him?" Bastien snapped.

A heavy tension fell across the table. Both men stared at him but said nothing.

The waiter returned when he noticed the guests and took their orders. It did nothing to break the tension at all. Even when he returned with the coffees, the discomfort was taut like a tight rope.

"Look," Luca said gently. "You didn't hear this from me..."

Gabriel released a sigh, as if Luca had just lit a firework.

"But some think you can't find Godric because...you don't want to."

Bastien released a laugh, but it wasn't a cute, playful laugh. It was dark and threatening, clipped and angry. "Like I would ever protect someone I hate so venomously."

"They say blood is thicker than water," Luca said.

"Put some red dye in water, and it looks the fucking same," Bastien said. "You can tell whatever asshole company you keep that I'm not protecting him. And you better not tell me who said that, because I'll fucking kill them."

I knew it wasn't an idle threat, not the way normal people teased each other with that phrase. This was completely real.

Luca stared at him for a moment. "President Martin."

The table fell into another bout of silence, but this one was heavier than all the others. A standoff happened between Bastien and Luca, both of them staring at each other and having a silent conversation.

The waiter arrived a moment later and placed the enormous platters of food in front of us, pancakes, eggs, bacon, and a scoop of baked beans. The hash browns were compacted into a ball rather than rolled flat, but they still looked good.

"Enough shop talk," Bastien said. "Let's fucking eat."

―――――――――

"You guys met at Silencio?" Luca asked, his attention on me.

"I'm a bartender there," I said. "Well, I was." On Monday, I would report for my new job at nine in the morning. It'd been a long time since I'd been up that early. I needed clothes for it, but I really didn't want to interact with Adrien at all.

"Where do you work now?" Luca's plate was completely empty because he ate every little piece, every damn crumb. They both ate like Bastien, like they were starving at every meal.

"Some investment company," I said, not wanting to admit that Bastien had hooked me up with the job.

"Some investment company?" Gabriel said with a laugh. "You don't know what it's called?"

"I gave her a job at the office," Bastien said. "You fucking pricks."

"Just trying to get to know your girlfriend a little better," Luca said.

"She's not my girlfriend," Bastien said.

I was both relieved by that interjection and simultaneously disappointed. I walked that line every moment I was in Bastien's presence. I'd never wanted a man more in my life, but that also marked him as the single most dangerous person in the world. The man who could burn down what little foundation I had left.

"Pussies have girlfriends. Men have women—and she's my woman."

He claimed me in no uncertain terms right in front of his boys. It was a turn-on, made me want to jump his bones right there in the booth, but I kept my eyes on the table and tried to be invisible. The warmth in my belly was quickly replaced by ice-cold fear.

Luca stared at Bastien for a long time, and a silent conversation passed between them.

What I wouldn't give to know the details.

The tab came, and all three men threw a hundred-euro-bill into the pile, even though brunch couldn't have possibly cost that much.

"We're going out tonight," Luca said. "You in?"

"Yeah, I'll be there," Bastien said.

Luca scooted out of the booth first. "Nice to meet you, Fleur."

"You too," I said quietly.

Gabriel gave me a nod before he walked out with Luca. They stepped onto the sidewalk, and then a black SUV appeared just like Bastien's. They disappeared from the curb and drove down the street.

Bastien pulled out his phone and texted his driver. "Ready, sweetheart?"

"Sure."

He opened the door for me and stepped onto the side-walk, sunshine visible between the buildings because it was a cloudless day, unusually warm for the spring. When he stood next to me, he was like the Eiffel Tower and I was the Seine. His friends were guys I would hit on in a bar, but they didn't hold a candle to the man beside me, with blue eyes that were warmer than a summer evening.

"Your friends were nice."

"They were assholes, and you know it." He looked down the street and saw his driver coming around the corner. "You want to come back to my place, or should I drop you off?"

It felt like a trick question. Was he inviting me back to his place to be polite, or did he actually want me there? He said he was honest to a fault, so I just asked. "What do you want me to do?"

"I want you to fuck me then take a nap with me."

I never had to wonder what he was thinking because he just told me—and that was refreshing. "Sounds good to me."

Chapter 14

Bastien

I sat at the bar and drank alone as I waited for Luca to get there.

He walked in a couple minutes later, wearing his leather jacket with his motorcycle helmet under his arm. He took the seat beside me and placed his helmet on the counter. He tapped his fingers against the bar to get the bartender's attention. "Gin and tonic."

The bartender threw his drink together and served it with a smile that asked for more than a tip.

"Thanks, sweetheart."

"No problem, babe." She walked away to serve the people who had been waiting at the bar a lot longer than Luca.

"Where's Gabriel?"

Luca shrugged before he took a drink. "I don't fucking know."

My fingers rested on the top of my glass, and I looked at my reflection in the mirror, saw the way Luca stared at the side of my face.

"So, you've got a woman now?"

"Is that a problem?" I turned in the swivel chair to look at him directly.

"She's still married."

"You act like she's having an affair."

"It is an affair—technically."

"Even if it were an affair, I wouldn't give a damn," I said. "And I don't give a damn that you don't like her."

"I never said I don't like her."

"You sure act like it." I took a drink.

"I just think you shouldn't get involved with a woman with so much baggage."

"I can lift a car—so I can carry her fucking baggage." I looked at the front of the bar again, seeing him stare at the side of my face in the mirror.

"When you called her your woman, she had this look on her face, like she didn't like it...or she was uncomfortable."

She could push me away all she wanted, but I would just pull tighter—like a fucking viper.

"Did you hear what I said—"

"What do you want from me, Luca?" I turned back to him. "I don't care that she's married. I don't care that she's getting divorced. I don't care if she says she's not ready for a relationship. She's my woman—period. You better get fucking used to it."

"You've never been with the same woman twice, and all of that changes for her? I get she's fucking hot with nice tits, but—"

"What the fuck did you just say?"

He raised his hand slightly then brought it down, like that would somehow decrease my ire. "I just don't want you to get fucked over, man. That's all. It's obvious this means more to you than it does to her because you're just a rebound."

I gave a quiet chuckle. "I'm not the rebound, Luca. I'm the gold fucking stallion."

"I can read people damn well. That's why no one will deal me in to poker anymore. And I see distance and restraint from her."

"You met her one time when she was ambushed by you idiots, and you think you know her?" I asked incredulously. "I know you're my boy and you're just looking out for me, but you need to step the fuck off, Luca."

He turned quiet and didn't continue to hound me with his ill opinion. He sat there and drank from his glass and let the tension start as a simmer and turn to a boil. It turned to steam and made the air humid.

He changed the subject. "I've asked my contacts about Godric. He doesn't sit still very long."

"I know."

"The longer he runs his game, the more he corrupts his order—"

"I know, Luca." My fingers rested around my glass.

"There's gotta be something."

I inhaled a slow breath. "I asked my mother." There was a separation of church and state, and I'd always honored it. Godric and I had very different interpretations of business and the law, and my mother refused to choose sides and favorites. She raised us to be this way, so she accepted our beliefs equally. But now, I needed her help if I was ever going to resolve it.

Luca stared at me for a long time, his hand on the glass without lifting it for a drink. "What did she say?"

"She'll think about it..."

He gave a slow nod. "You think that will work?"

"I don't fucking know, man. It's been a long time since I talked to him."

"Even if she agrees, he probably won't."

"Right." I took a drink from my glass, and now, there was nothing but ice cubes left behind.

He faced the bar and the mirror and drank in silence.

We sat there together, both of us thinking about the thorn in our sides, the man I called my brother.

Then my phone vibrated with a text. It could be anyone because my phone went off all hours of the night, but there was only one person I hoped it would be. I'd just seen her this morning, but I wouldn't mind coming home to her in my bed, her legs wrapped around my waist while she whispered my name.

But it was my mother. ***I'll do it.***

It was ten in the evening when my driver pulled up to the gates.

My heart was still, my pulse steady. I was on the precipice of what I wanted, but I knew just because it was close didn't mean it was within my grasp. This meeting could have the opposite effect I desired—and just make things worse.

I checked in with her security and was led into the house.

She warned me that the element of surprise would only last a minute because his security would inform him of my arrival before I reached the dining room. Instead of being a polite guest and waiting for the butler to escort me, I walked myself through the house to the dining room located at the back.

I heard my mother's quiet laugh before I rounded the corner.

He was at the head of the table like it was his fucking house, blond hair and blue eyes. He sprang into action right away, rising to his feet and pulling his gun out of the back of his jeans and aiming at me within a second. The laughter and merriment of dinner quickly evaporated when the tension set in. Music played from the sound system, but it was masked by the tension.

I'd honored my mother's request and had come unarmed, but he had no such honor.

"Godric." Mother rose to her feet and pressed her hand down on his arm.

It didn't budge. In fact, he cocked it.

She gripped the opening of the barrel. "Put it down."

My brother's face was contorted in restrained rage, treating me like a hit man who'd murdered his entire family for a cheap paycheck. He had a structured jawline like I did, the same eyes. There was no doubt we were of the same parentage. After a furious standoff, he lowered the gun.

Mother twisted it from his fingers and confiscated it before clicking the safety. "Bring a gun to dinner again, and I'll bend you over my knee and spank you like a child." She slammed the gun onto the table next to her soup bowl. The table was long enough to fit fifteen guests comfortably, but it was just the two of them together near the window.

Godric's stare remained latched on mine. He was in a long-sleeved shirt, so the ink on his arms was hidden from view. He was tall like I was, muscular because he lifted every morning and night, always determined to be bigger than me. "I trusted you, Mother. That won't happen again."

"Trust hasn't been betrayed," she said. "My only desire is for my sons to speak to each other."

He turned his gaze on her, his rage restrained. "You set me up—"

"I want my sons to speak to each other."

He gave her a furious stare before he turned away from the table, kicking his chair hard and making it tip over then slide across the rug. "Alright, let's talk." He raised his voice to a yell so all the staff throughout the house could hear. "What does this shithead have to say?"

I was still on the other side of the room, looking at my brother thirty feet away, standing in the dining room that had vaulted ceilings twenty feet in the air. The curtains were pulled away from the windows, showing the lights of the city outside, the drops of rain that stuck to the glass.

"Speak, boy." He gave a loud whistle, calling me like a dog.

Mother gave a quiet sigh as she watched this derail before it even could start down the track.

I knew he was pissed that his own mother had personally bested him, and like a child, he was throwing a tantrum. I moved to the sitting area and took a seat in one of the cushioned armchairs. I crossed one ankle on the opposite knee then gestured to the other armchair for him to sit.

He stared at me, his breaths visible in the way his chest rose and fell. He walked past the table, snatched the water glass off the surface, and threw it against the wall on his way, missing my head by a few inches. It shattered, and water soaked into the rug.

I didn't react.

Godric dropped into the armchair across from me, his

forearms on his knees as he leaned forward, giving me that lethal stare.

Moments passed. The music continued to play overhead.

The butler and guards entered the room to investigate the commotion. Someone turned off the sound system.

We continued to stare each other down.

Mother approached us near the coffee table, wearing black trousers and a tweed vest, a coat hanger draped in jewelry. With her hands together at her waist, she looked at us both. "I only have one son at any time, and I would like to have two. There is nothing more sacred than the blood you two share, the blood of emperors, the blood of power. It's a shame to waste this life as opponents rather than allies." She looked at each of us before she grabbed the gun off the dining table and exited the room.

The silence was deafening, so stagnant it made the air stale. I stared at blue eyes identical to my own but saw a man who couldn't be more different in every way that mattered. We used to get along as kids, but once we became adults, our morals and politics ripped us apart like a thin sheet of paper.

He didn't speak, just continued to stare me down like a cockroach he needed to squash.

"It's just a conversation."

"A conversation that won't change anything—and therefore, a waste of time." He sat back and slouched into the chair, his elbow propped on the armrest with his closed fist against his hard chin. "A fucking waste of time."

"I don't want it to be this way."

"You aren't the only one who shares that sentiment."

"Godric—"

"How long do you think this will last? Policing those who can't be policed. Making rules for the lawless and ungoverned. How long do you think it'll be before your body dangles from a crane over Notre-Dame? You say it's about morality, but it can't be if you're directly profiting from it."

"You know how much money they save when they don't have to hide their transports? When they pass straight through customs? When they load their shipments onto the docks in broad daylight? Time and money, all saved under the Fifth Republic. They save far more money than what they pay in taxes."

"Perhaps," he said. "But the cost of labor has diminished their profits considerably."

"Well, that's too fucking bad," I snapped. "A million euros poorer, what a fucking tragedy."

"It's a lot more than a million—"

"Still inconsequential."

"Easy for you to say when you're pulling in a million per day...on average."

"I'm sure you make a lot more than that, Godric."

"The money matters, but it doesn't matter as much as the principle of it. We run our businesses as we see fit, and following the rules of some pompous little prick is a load of bullshit. You have your beliefs and that's fucking fine, but the rest of us don't. Don't make carnivores eat asparagus just because you're a goddamn vegetarian."

"You're going to compare women to asparagus?" I asked in disbelief. "They're fucking people, Godric—"

He shot forward to the edge of his seat. "I don't give a shit. Look at me." His eyes were stretched wide, and the veins in his neck popped from the strain. "Does it look like I give a shit? Does it?"

"These are daughters—"

"These are fucking nobodies, Bastien. The homeless, the poor, women stupid enough to walk through a bad neighborhood alone at two in the morning—"

"So, they deserve this?"

He gave a shrug.

"That's it? That's all you have to say?"

"It's how the world works, Bastien."

"But it doesn't have to—and it's not going to."

He returned his chin to his hard knuckles and stared at me. "Why do you care so much, Bastien?"

"Do I need a reason?"

"I think you do when you risk a knife to your back. You think you have control of this city, but a lot of men want you dead."

"Doesn't seem that way to me." No one had tried to come for me, not in my home, not on the street, not at any of the functions of the Senate. Maybe they wanted me dead, but actually executing a plan was a different story.

Godric stared in silence, his eyes locked on my face with the stillness of a statue.

"Godric, you can get into another line of business. It doesn't have to be this way—"

"It does, Bastien."

"You're telling me, when we were kids, your dream was to be a human trafficker?" I asked incredulously. "Because I remember all you ever wanted to be was a veterinarian."

Godric burst with laughter. "I forgot about that."

"You wanted to help animals, and now, you steal women from their homes. That's who you want to be, Godric?"

"Anything you say before puberty doesn't count."

"Answer the question."

His laughter died away, and he turned serious once more. "Bastien, I don't care. I don't care about anyone or anything—besides myself. You can try to guilt me with your questions and your exasperation, but you can't guilt someone who lacks a conscience."

I gave a shake of my head. "I don't believe that."

He shrugged. "People change, Bastien. Boys become men. We stop caring about animals and toys and obsess over money and pussy. It's just how it is."

My brother and I had been divided a long time, but I was still disappointed by the words I heard.

"Bastien." His voice turned serious, his stare losing all hint of humor.

I met his look.

"The Fifth Republic will fall. The old order will return. And you can't stop it." His cheek was propped on his closed knuckles again, his somber eyes watching me across the table. "I suggest you embrace the old order to save your neck—or step down and let someone else take your place. Take my advice."

"That sounds like a threat."

"I guess you wouldn't know." He continued to stare at me, the coffee table between us. "I may not like you, but that doesn't mean I want you dead."

"I thought you didn't care about anyone but yourself."

"I care about Mom. Though, not so much right now. And she'd be ticked if I let you get shanked in the street." He looked past me out the window, his eyes lingering on the city we seemed to own together, just under different leaderships. "I'm not going to change, and if you aren't going to change, this only ends one way—with one of us dead." His eyes came back to me. "And it's not going to be me, Bastien."

I met with Roger at Chez Georges. We had dinner together like civilized people, but we talked shop the entire time, not caring about the people who sat directly next to us and overheard the entire thing. I didn't eat bread very often, but Chez Georges had the best bread in Paris, and I enjoyed that more than my steak.

He got a call from his wife toward the end of dinner and had to leave in a rush, so I sat there alone and finished my meal, preferring the solitude anyway. We discussed what we needed to discuss, so finishing dinner together was just an obligation.

A woman dropped into Roger's chair across from me, wearing a pink floral dress with a gold necklace around her throat. She was a pretty brunette, looked to be in her early twenties, which was a bit too young for me. "I thought you could use some company since your guest left."

My eyes moved to the empty seat from which she originated. Another young woman was there, probably a friend or a sister. She drank her wine as she watched her companion make a move on me.

"My name is Abigail."

My eyes moved back to my new guest, annoyed that she was there, but also annoyed that the woman getting my dick continued to keep me at arm's length. Told me she wanted casual, but if it was casual, I would be fucking this woman and whoever else I met on the way—and I knew she wouldn't like that one bit.

Not that I wanted to fuck anyone else...

If this woman were older, I would give her a cold reception, but since she was young, I decided to preserve her self-esteem. "I'm too old for you—and I'm married."

"Oh...you aren't wearing a ring."

"I'm not the kind of guy to wear one."

The disappointment crept into her pretty features, washing away her joy like the rising tide destroyed a sandcastle on the beach. "I'll let you enjoy your dinner." She scooted out of the chair and went back to her table.

I returned to my steak, listening to the conversations at all the nearby tables, talking about new decorations for the home, upcoming doctor's appointments, the horrible traffic in the city. Mundane bullshit.

My phone lit up on the table. *I like my new job. It's nice to be home by five rather than go to work at five.*

Her messages normally brought a smile to my face, but my mood was sour. Had been sour since my unproductive conversation with Godric last night. *Good.* I'd forgotten that she'd started at the office that day. Was too busy with my own shit to think about anything else.

The divorce papers were approved by the judge. Now we set a date for a hearing.

You only went to a hearing for a divorce if the spouses couldn't agree on the division of assets, so I wasn't sure what Adrien was contesting. Unless he was picking a fight to draw out the divorce as long as possible just to be a dick. Seemed like something he would do. *Good, things are moving.* I ate the last few scraps of my steak then asked for the tab.

How are you?

Been better.

May I ask why?

Just bullshit at work.

You say that a lot.

Because it's true. Some days were calm, but those days were few and far between. Collecting tariffs and keeping dealers and distributors in line was an immense task. There were a lot of weapons and drugs to move in and out of France, and it was my job to oversee all that and make sure tariffs were being paid on all of it. And then I had to go up against my own brother and decide how I would remove him from power without killing him. He deserved to die for all the shit he'd done, but when it came time to squeeze the trigger, my finger wouldn't move.

I would love to see you…if you're up for it.

I was already out the door and waiting for my driver at the curb. *I'll be there in a few.*

Good. I miss you.

I smirked before I slid the phone back into my pocket. For a woman who only wanted casual, she acted the opposite. Her texts used to be rare and infrequent, but now she texted me on a daily basis.

I hopped into the SUV and headed to her apartment a couple blocks away. When the driver dropped me off, the café was full of people having dinner inside and on the outside patio. People biked and walked down the cobble-stones to the *église Saint-Eustache* or the mall farther down the street. Only in Paris could you find an ancient cathedral right next to a modern mall with a McDonald's and a Claire's.

I let myself into her apartment because she'd shared the code with me weeks back. The elevator had finally been fixed, but I took the stairs anyway because I could barely fit in the tiny enclosure. I made it to her door and let myself inside, moving down the winding hallway until I reached her main room, the dining room and living room a single space.

I stilled when I saw her—standing in nothing but a tiny black G-string.

Mother of god.

The lights were dimmed and a few candles were lit to set the mood, but all I cared about was the fine woman with the tits I was about to suck raw. Her brown hair was soft and around her shoulders, and she had that look in her eyes that showed how much she wanted me even though I was fully clothed.

I reached behind my head and pulled my shirt over my back before I tossed it onto one of the chairs. When I moved into her, one of her arms hooked around my neck, and she cupped my face, her lips parting to take the hungry kiss that was coming.

I clenched her tight ass in my hand before I lifted her into me so I didn't have to bend my neck to kiss her. She weighed nothing to me, soft and light like a beautiful breeze on a spring day. Her kiss was fire on my mouth, desperate for my passion. She dug her fingers into my hair as she kissed me. "I fucking missed you." She spoke to me between her kisses, her voice breathless.

Fuck, the things this woman did to me.

"Bastien." She said my name like she'd been desperate to say it all day, like it was hanging on the edge of her tongue.

I carried her to the small bedroom and threw her on the bed.

She gave a cry when she bounced, but her eyes were lit up with that same intense passion only I could satisfy.

I'd never taken off my pants so fast. Boots were kicked off. Boxers were down and on the hardwood floor.

She stared at me like I was the finest piece of meat she'd ever seen.

I grabbed her hips and dragged her to the edge of the bed before I hooked my fingers into that little black thong and tugged it free. Then I slid my arms underneath her thighs and opened her wide to kiss that aching pussy.

She let out a cry as she arched her back. "God..."

I fucked her with my mouth, sucked her clit hard between my lips and made her wince, worshipped that pussy for the perfection that it was. I loved her taste, loved the way she was wet before I made any effort to make her that way. I didn't go down on a woman for a one-night stand, but I was happy to get on my knees and stick my face between her sexy thighs. I could do this all fucking night.

She dug her fingers into my hair, and she rocked her hips against me, grinding her sex right into my face because it felt damn good. Her pants and cries rose, her hips bucking harder. "Stop..."

I sucked her clit and lips hard into my mouth.

She moaned again. "Wait...don't make me come."

I smiled against her pussy. "That's the first time I've heard that."

She lifted herself on her arms and dragged her body away before she opened her knees wide, beckoning my hips to slide in between her soft thighs. "I only want to come with you inside me." Her sex gleamed from my kisses. It was red from how hard I'd sucked on her.

This was the only woman who made my dick twitch like a fucking slingshot. I moved over the bed on top of her and slid between her thighs, my dick smashing through her entrance and sliding deep inside in a single motion.

She moaned in my ear and clawed at my back as she folded underneath me.

I pounded into her with the pace of a sprinting horse, my face pressed close to hers, watching her eyes collect tears because she was about to come. "Come, sweetheart. Come all over my dick."

Her pussy tightened before she cried out, squeezing the tears from the corners of her eyes and making them streak down her cheeks. Her nails dug into me, and she panted and cried as she felt the enormous explosion inside her little pussy. "Bastien..." She already boosted my ego enough, but saying my name was the cherry on the sundae.

I felt the slickness increase, felt all the cream she made for me. It coated my dick to the balls. "I love this pussy." Pussy had all been the same to me, tight and wet and the perfect hole for my hard dick, but her pussy was a fucking rose garden in Versailles. It was the queen of pussies, worthy of a crown made of gold and rubies, the only place my dick ever wanted to go. I fisted her hair and gripped it like a leash before I pressed my face to her cheek. "I fucking love this pussy."

Chapter 15

Fleur

Be there in 10 mins.

I took a breath when I saw his message, standing in the black dress with the enormous slit up the thigh. It was the most expensive piece of clothing I owned at the moment, straight from Versace. I paired it with heels from Saint Laurent. I wore a diamond necklace, but it was fake, and I hoped no one would be snooty enough to notice the difference.

I hadn't wanted to spend more of his money, so I hadn't bought a coat to go with it. I would just be cold during the walk from the car to the entry doors. And I could always move in closer to Bastien if I needed warmth.

I left the apartment and stepped out of the double doors to the building. It was a Saturday evening, so the sidewalk was packed with people heading to dinner or drinks. My heels were wobbly on the cobblestone as I made it to the edge of the sidewalk.

The SUV rounded the corner and came to a stop in front of me.

Bastien appeared in a tuxedo, his blond hair slicked back, looking like a million bucks.

More like a billion.

He stepped out, and he looked me over appreciatively. "Money well spent." He nodded for me to step inside, and when I did, he gave me a gentle spank on the ass. He climbed into the chair beside me then moved his hand to my thigh, his fingertips just underneath my dress, his arm so big and long that he could reach across the aisle with ease.

I opened my clasp and pulled out the remaining bills that I hadn't spent. "This is what was left over."

He didn't even look at it. "Keep it."

"Bastien." I continued to hold out the cash because all I wanted from him was him, not his money. I'd only bought these things because I had to. They would sit in my closet and probably never be worn again because I didn't have the lifestyle to support it.

He gave a sigh before he took the cash and shoved it in the pocket behind the driver's seat, probably because it was too thick to place in his wallet or he really just didn't care about the money at all. His hand returned to my thigh, his fingers higher up my dress until he touched my panties underneath.

He looked out the window.

I watched the side of his face, studied the hardness of his jawline, the cords that popped in his neck, all the features that revved my engine louder than the SUV we rode in. His pretty eyes were a contradiction to the rest of him, the only softness he possessed. His jaw was clean because he shaved for the event, and he wore a black watch on his wrist, something I'd never seen him wear before.

"Any pointers?" I asked.

He turned back to look at me. "Just be yourself."

"Then I'm going to be a dumb girl who doesn't know shit about politics."

He smirked. "I'm not bringing you to talk about politics."

"Then why are you bringing me?"

His blue eyes continued to look into mine, to spear my soul with their subtle intensity. "Because you're my woman." Like everything else he said, he said it with confidence, not the least bit concerned that I would correct him.

I had been more than somebody's woman once. I had been their wife—and they'd cheated on me for years. I'd trusted that man implicitly, wouldn't have thought it for a second, didn't find his late nights out remotely suspicious—and I'd been made a fool.

I didn't want to be a fool ever again.

He seemed to read the hesitancy in my gaze because he followed it with, "I said what I said."

———

We pulled up to Luxembourg Palace, a place I'd only seen from passing by in a cab, and Bastien got out first before he took my hand and helped me step out in the sky-high heels. Instead of moving his hand to the small of my back or not touching me at all, he continued to hold my hand as we crossed the pathway over the manicured lawn and approached the three-story palace made of stone.

We were ushered into the ballroom with a crowd of people, chandeliers hanging from the ceiling while waiters offered flutes of champagne and canapés. It was an enormous room, the perfect size to hold a wedding with five hundred guests. Tables were covered in champagne-pink tablecloths with enormous centerpieces filled with tall lilies. A four-piece quartet played music from the corner, and the men were dressed in tuxedos and the women in beautiful gowns.

But none of the men or women were as beautiful as Bastien. He was a towering man with his height, and he carried his muscular body with a stiffness that showed the hardness of his spine. His composure was relaxed, like he was in his element in a room full of the aristocracy. A waiter passed by, and he grabbed a flute of champagne for me.

"Thank you." I took a drink and noticed he didn't take one for himself.

It wasn't long after that that the mingling began. Men who were obviously acquainted with Bastien came over for small talk, jokes about other people not in the vicinity, and a bit of politics.

Bastien kept his hand on the small of my back as he introduced me. "This is my woman, Fleur. Fleur, these are some of the members of the Senate." He introduced each one of them by name, even remembering the names of their wives, who hardly said two words.

I'd told him I wanted to keep it casual, and just as I'd assumed, he basically disregarded what I'd requested. I was whisked away into a relationship that I hadn't agreed to, and that meant there were expectations and a certain degree of trust, trust that I'd never consented to give.

Bastien was a man of the shadows, a man who would always be committed to his work above everything else, a bad boy who killed people for a living. Adrien was a normal guy I'd thought I could trust, so Bastien was even less trustworthy.

How had I ended up exactly where I didn't want to be?

We took our seats at a table, the seating chart on a big poster in the entryway, and we were surrounded by boring and pretentious men from the Senate and National Assembly—but Luca was also there with his date.

Luca gave me a cold reception, a nod in acknowledgment of my existence. "This is Diana." He gestured to the woman with him, a beautiful brunette who looked like she belonged in a magazine or on a fashion billboard. Far too beautiful to be introduced only by her name. Luca and his date went to the bar to grab something stronger than the champagne distributed on the tables.

"Your friend doesn't like me."

Bastien's hand went to my thigh under the table. "He doesn't like anybody."

I appreciated that he didn't lie to me, but the truth still stung a little bit. "That seems to be true, considering the way he treats his girlfriend."

"She's not his girlfriend."

"Then who is she?"

He shrugged. "A woman he has in his pocket."

"Why bring someone anyway?"

"It's all about optics. You earn more respect if you've got a beautiful woman on your arm."

"Do I earn you respect? Because I'm not the bombshell she is."

Bastien scoffed, a handsome smile on his face. "She's so thin you can see her hip bones through her dress and the vertebrae up her spine—and her tits are fake. You, on the other hand, are the finest piece of woman I've ever seen." He moved his arm over the back of my chair and gave me that intense gaze that could win him any hand in poker. "I'll take you to my office and prove it."

I felt the heat burn underneath my skin, bringing a sting to my cheeks. I broke eye contact when his confidence made my strength shatter. I'd never felt safer with anyone, but that also made me feel more vulnerable in numerous ways.

"Stop doing that."

I turned back to him. "What?"

"I take a step forward, you take a step back," he said. "We've done it at least ten times now."

My heart started to race when I realized his actions were completely intentional. When I told him how I felt, it wasn't what he wanted to hear, so he disregarded it. "I need to use the restroom." I left my chair and crossed the ballroom until I exited through the double doors. The bathrooms were located in the main entryway, so I took my time walking there, taking advantage of the moment to process the adrenaline that pounded in my heart.

The bathroom was empty and I didn't need to use the toilet, so I took a seat in one of the armchairs near the vanity where women could touch up their makeup. I sat there and crossed my legs, taking a break from the invisible pressure Bastien applied to me.

I sat there for a couple minutes, knowing I shouldn't linger too long. Otherwise, he would come looking for me. Wouldn't be surprised if he let himself in to the women's restroom to check. I looked in the mirror and fixed my hair before I stepped back into the main room.

I halted when I came face-to-face with the man I wanted to avoid.

His eyes weren't intense the way they had been before, so possessive they were physical. Now, they were just angry, blue flames in those pretty eyes. "Let me explain to you what casual is. Casual is a random text from someone you haven't seen in two weeks, asking for a hookup. Casual is wearing a condom. Casual is fucking several people at once. Casual is *not* texting me every day, is *not* telling me you miss me, *not* sleeping over and having pancakes the next morning. So, what do you want from me, sweetheart?" He didn't raise his voice, but his tone was so powerful it felt like he screamed. "Because I haven't been with anyone else since the first time I saw you, but I can change that as soon as tonight if you'd like."

I inhaled a sharp breath like he'd slapped me.

"I asked you a question."

"Stop yelling at me."

"You think this is yelling?" He cocked his head slightly, his eyes growing angrier.

"Don't threaten me."

"Do you want me to fuck other people or not?"

I stormed off, heading to the main door so I could get out of there.

He grabbed me by the arm and yanked me back to him with immense force, like I weighed nothing to him. "You can leave when this is finished." He stepped in my way as he let me go, his back to the main doors, the security guys pretending like they didn't notice the commotion.

"I told you I'm not looking for anything serious right now. I'm not even divorced yet—"

"Are you over him?"

"What?"

"You heard what I said." He crowded me. "Are you still hung up on the little bitch who stabbed you in the back?"

"No." I'd left our home heartbroken, but the depth of Adrien's deception was so deep that I couldn't feel anything for him. All the love I'd had for that man just died. I'd realized I didn't know the man I was married to.

"Then what is the problem?" He continued to speak to me in a vicious tone, like I was the one in the wrong when he wouldn't respect my boundaries.

"I told you I'm not ready for anything serious, and you're going around telling people that I'm your woman."

"*You are my woman,*" he snapped. "You fuck my brains out and hold on to me all night like I'm your goddamn teddy bear. Is it normal for you to go around town and fuck random guys without wearing anything if you aren't their woman?"

"No—"

"Have you fucked anyone else since we met?"

I couldn't even imagine it. "No..."

His stare pierced mine for several hard seconds. "Do you want me to sleep with other people?"

I refused to answer, refused to dig this hole deeper.

"Your poker face is shit, you know that?" He clenched his jaw tighter when I didn't answer. But then it slowly relaxed, his eyes shifting back and forth between mine as he read me like words on a white page. "You're scared."

My lungs sucked in a gulp of air, his fingers finding the wound and digging deep.

"I'm not him."

My eyes flicked away, the button to my trigger tapped.

"I'm not him."

I was forced to look at him again, gripped by the power of his voice.

"I understand you're coming out of a long-term relationship that ended in a dumpster fire. I understand you haven't had time to heal everything he's broken. But I'm not asking you to marry me or move in with me or do anything you don't want to do. But I won't be disrespected either. You're either in this with me, or I'm gone."

I swallowed because the idea of losing him was devastating.

His eyes shifted back and forth between mine. "I'm your man—and you're my fucking woman. Period. Do you understand me?" His ruthless eyes continued to burn into mine with the viciousness of a mountain lion.

"I—I don't want to get hurt again." Self-loathing washed over me, hating myself for allowing myself to be weak in front of another person. I only showed the depth of my despair to myself—and myself alone.

He sheathed his tone slightly. "I would never hurt you, sweetheart."

"You're dangerous. You kill people. You're not the kind of man to commit to a woman for long. You aren't the kind of man to get married or have children—"

"You're making a lot of assumptions."

"Am I wrong? I saw you in that bar, and I wanted you. And you've been the greatest high I've ever known. I've wanted time to stand still so we can be this way forever, but I know it can't stay like this and it's going to end and I don't want to get my hopes up. So when you say shit like I'm your woman, you're just making it harder—"

"Why does it have to end?"

"Because you're going to get tired of me and replace me with someone else. Because you'll meet a girl at a bar, and I'll disappear from your mind. You'll tell me how much I mean to you and then turn around and stick your dick in someone else." I felt the hot tears in the back of my eyes, feeling so fucking worthless, feeling all the damage Adrien had caused. "And then I'll be crushed again, crushed more than I am right now. It's just easy to keep things casual, to make sure that I have no expectations, that I don't trust you, so you can't hurt me the way he crushed me." The tears came and slipped down my cheeks, and I was fucking humiliated.

"Sweetheart." His voice was gentle like a fall breeze. His hands were on me, one on my cheek so his thumb could wipe the fallen tear. His lips caught the other while he buried his hand in my hair. "It's gonna be okay."

I kept my eyes closed and grabbed his wrist with both hands, remembering the night he'd come to the bar and held my hand and said the same words. As long as my eyes shut out the world, I wouldn't have to face it. I could hide until it went away.

He waited for me to look at him again on my own. "Sweetheart."

"I—I'm not ready to be in a relationship."

"Look at me."

"No..."

"I know how brave you are," he said quietly. "Look at me."

I took a breath before I opened my eyes, feeling how wet they were when they were exposed to the air.

He continued to look down at me, his eyes soft and kind.

"If I walked away right now and took someone else home, would it hurt you?"

Just the thought made my heart drop into my stomach. I couldn't answer the question with words, so I just nodded.

"Then it's too late to turn back," he said. "So, be with me."

I'd ended up in the corner I tried to evade—and I was fucking terrified.

"I've been yours since the moment I saw you. Now be mine."

"I'm so fucking scared—"

"I'm just asking you to acknowledge what we already are. It doesn't need to go further than that. We can take this as slow as you want. We can stay this way forever if that's what you want. But I can't do this if you won't give me the respect I deserve. So, give me what I want—you—or I walk."

My eyes were focused on his chin and neck, staring at the hard muscles of his jawline and neck. My hands continued to grip his wrist as I felt his palm against my cheek. "I don't want to lose you."

"Then you're mine. Say it."

My eyes remained down.

His palm lifted my chin and forced my stare to his. "*Say it.*"

I got lost in those blue eyes every time I looked at them. Got lost in this man whenever he walked through the door. He was the sexiest man I'd ever met, and the second he walked into my life, he set everything on fire and I burned in his flames. "You're mine...and I'm yours."

He didn't ask me where I wanted to go. Just decided we would go to his place.

After our fight, we'd returned to our seats at the table, and he was all over me, his hand either on my thigh, draped over the back of the chair, or he kissed me right in front of everyone, *really* kissed me, not an innocent peck on the lips.

He gave me his jacket when he knew I was cold, so I sat there and drowned in the material, his big hand so far up my dress that his fingers were hooked into my panties. His resentment evaporated after the fight, and now he wanted me even more when the barriers were removed.

I knew I'd just gotten myself into a precarious position, in a relationship with a man whom I knew I should

287

avoid. If I hadn't just been looking for good sex with a hot guy, I would have steered clear of him in the first place. But as the weeks passed and I got attached, deeply attached, my nails so deep under the skin they hit bone, I'd sealed my fate. Now, I was in a relationship with the most dangerous man in Paris.

We entered his home and took the elevator to the top floor to his bedroom. When we walked inside, his butler had already started the fire in the fireplace and placed a tray of dessert and champagne on the table for us to enjoy.

Bastien immediately undressed like he was anxious to get rid of all the clothing, the suspenders over his shoulders, the trousers, the bow tie around his thick neck. He unbuttoned his white shirt and yanked it off his big arms until his true form was revealed, bare skin over bulging muscles and marked in black ink. He left everything on the floor like it was Gerard's problem to deal with tomorrow. He stood in just his boxers, the cotton taut over his tight ass, the powerful muscles hugging his spine.

I was still cold from standing outside waiting for our driver in the long line of cars, so I moved to the fire while wearing his jacket, letting the heat warm my frozen skin.

He stepped out of the bedroom a moment later, his blond hair still slicked back, his eyes sharp like he wasn't the least bit tired from all the small talk and networking bullshit. "I can warm you up, sweetheart." He returned to the bedroom without waiting for my answer.

I followed him a second later, placing his jacket over the armchair before I slipped off my heels. When I flattened my feet against the floor, I let out a moan, my toes releasing all the pain they'd been harboring all night. I unzipped the dress and delicately placed it over the chair so it wouldn't wrinkle.

I'd barely turned toward the bed when I smacked into his hard chest like a concrete wall. His big hands gripped my ass, and he lifted me into him, the warmth of his body matching the fire in the other room. He carried me to the bed as he stared into my eyes. Instead of throwing me onto the mattress, he rolled me onto my back and moved over me, his thick body warmer than any blanket. He positioned me underneath him before he hooked his thumbs into the straps of my black thong and pulled it free. He was already naked, his dick hard like it'd been all night, every time he pressed against me.

He folded me underneath him, locking both of his wrists behind my knees before he ground his length over my sex and rubbed it against my clit, his hungry dick harder than any vibrator I'd ever used. His blue eyes were on me, watching my reaction to him, enjoying the sight of me below him. "You're holding yourself back. Why?" The man had eyes that could see through walls, pierce through hearts.

It was easier to embrace him with passion when I could lie to myself, when I could say it meant nothing, when I knew it would end and I was okay with it. But now, I was very aware of the way I felt for him, that the moment I lost him, I would be devastated. "Because I'm scared..."

"Why?" He brought his face closer to mine, our lips almost touching. He continued to grind into me, smearing himself in the arousal that he squeezed from my slit.

I cupped his face in my hands as I looked into his pretty but hard blue eyes, those of a man who had taken all of me at first glance, who had become a lifeline when I drowned in the Atlantic alone. "Because you're too good to be true."

Something like that would usually make him smirk playfully, with a hint of arrogance, but the smile never came. Instead, he continued his hard stare before he shifted his attention to my lips. He closed the distance and kissed me softly, the softest kiss he'd ever given me. A light touch of our mouths. A gentle embrace from a rugged giant. The slowness continued as he shifted his hips and guided the head of his dick to my folds. He found the entrance to my slit and sank in as he kept kissing me, his dick pushing through my tightness until he stopped before I became uncomfortable with too much of his length.

He started to rock into me as his kisses continued, our bodies moving together with aching languidness, like this was my first time ever and he was handling it like a gentleman. His kisses became more passionate and possessive, and soon, he devoured me as his thrusts grew in intensity. He lifted himself over me, his wrists still locked behind my knees, pounding into me with even strokes.

I gripped his forearms as I felt him stretch me over and over, the biggest dick that had ever been inside me. I panted and moaned, the slickness starting and contin-uing between my legs, dripping down my crack to his sheets below. I already wanted to come, and my body tightened in preparation for it, knowing it was looming over the horizon. Adrien had made me come most of the time, but there were plenty of times when it didn't happen because I wasn't feeling it or the position didn't feel right...lots of reasons. But with Bastien, he delivered every single time, multiple times.

"Fuck, I love watching you come."

I wasn't quite there, but he somehow knew I was right on the edge. He could read my body, read the heat in my eyes, feel the tightness that squeezed him with an iron grip. His words, his voice, the sexy look on his face, made me come and shed tears that trailed down my cheeks. My hips tried to buck against him but his wrists kept me in place, and he increased his pace at my enthusiasm, his chest turning red from a flush of arousal. "Bastien…"

"You're my woman. *Say it.*"

I didn't hesitate, swept up in the blissful throes of passion that scorched me from head to toe. "I'm your woman," I said breathlessly.

"Damn right, you are." He fucked me harder, pumping into me and giving me his full length, finishing me off while he reached his end. The sexiest moan came from his clenched jaw, his pumps suddenly slowing down as he began to fill me with the load he'd carried in his barrel all night. "This pussy is fucking mine."

He slowed down until he came to a stop, his dick still hard and stiff inside me. He dropped his head and kissed me again, kissed the corner of my mouth and then my neck, blanketing me with his affection, the sweat from his skin, his smell. Then he began again, fucking me hard right from the start, folding me even more underneath him, his balls tapping against my ass as he screwed me like he hadn't just done so. "Mine."

When I woke up the next morning, it was raining.

I could hear it against the roof, hear it pelt the windows. I listened to it for a while, treasuring the peace it brought me as

I slowly regained consciousness. When I found the strength to open my eyes, I looked at my world, saw the curtains closed over the windows. My phone was on the nightstand, and I tapped the screen, seeing it was already after noon.

Fuck, I really slept.

Bastien wasn't there, which wasn't surprising. He'd probably already worked out, showered, and had breakfast. I got out of bed, stole one of his shirts from his drawer, then opened the doors to the other room.

The fire burned in the hearth, and the TV showed a game, Manchester United versus Southampton. Bastien was in just his sweatpants on the couch, watching the game intently like he had money on it. "Fucking twats don't know how to kick a damn ball." He must have already eaten because he had a glass of scotch in front of him.

I stepped farther into the room. "Morning. Or afternoon, I guess."

When he turned to look at me, the annoyance over the progress of the game immediately evaporated. "It's a beautiful morning whenever you walk into the room." He wore the most handsome smile as he left the couch and came to me. His thick arm circled me and brought me close as he kissed me hard on the mouth. Then he gave my ass a hard squeeze and a playful spank. "Pancakes?"

"You haven't eaten?"

"I already had breakfast. Couldn't wait."

"Then don't worry about getting me anything."

"I need to eat lunch anyway. So, pancakes or something more traditional?"

It was past one. I'd already taken up most of his day hanging around. "I should get going, so don't worry about me."

He stilled, his soft stare slowly hardening to the blunt side of a hammer. "It's Sunday. You have somewhere to be?"

"No. I just want to get out of your hair—"

"Let me save you some time," he snapped. "If I want you to leave, I'll tell you. Alright?"

"I assumed that you have plans or work."

"And if that's the case, I'll tell you." He was a teddy bear one moment, then a fire-breathing dragon the next. "I want you here in my t-shirt on the couch, watching TV in front of the fire, fucking in the armchair, napping whenever we feel like it, and having Gerard bring us whatever the fuck we want. Is that a problem?"

"Stop yelling at me."

"You'll never know what I sound like when I yell because I would never yell at you," he said. "You're my goddamn woman, so start acting like it. I want you here—always. Live here for all I fucking care." He continued to stare me down with a jawline that was as sharp as the edge of a blade. "You understand me?"

I didn't know how a man who was so drop-dead gorgeous could possibly want me so much. Who didn't play games, who just told me how he felt when he felt it. He could be fucking all of Paris, but he'd settled for me. "Yes..."

"Then get your ass over here."

I moved back into him, seeing the way his angry eyes watched me the whole way. I rose on my tiptoes and extended my hand for the back of his neck, as far as I could reach. My body was lifted by his strong arms, and I was face-to-face with him, his big hands gripping my ass. My arms circled his neck, and I pressed my forehead to his. "I'll take the pancakes."

A slow smile crept over his lips before he pulled away to look me in the eye. He was so hot when he looked intense, even pissed off. But when he smiled...it was like the most handsome he looked. His eyes shone like the water of the Mediterranean, and he was warmer than the Tuscan sun. "That's my girl."

Bastien and Fleur's story continues in ***The Carver***.

Fifth Republic Special Editions

I'm so excited to announce the Fifth Republic Special Editions! These stunning hardcovers are designed for diehard fans like you. Preorder now at this link!

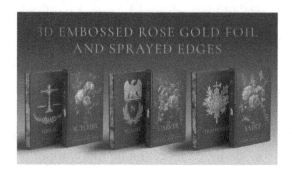